Adrian Duncan is an Irish arti[...]
novel *Love Notes from a Germ[...]
2019 John McGahern Book P[...]
Sabbatical in Leipzig (2020) [...]
Kerry Group Irish Novel of the Year. His collection
of short stories *Midfield Dynamo* was published
in 2021 and longlisted for the Edge Hill Prize. His
third novel, *The Geometer Lobachevsky*, was published
in April 2022.

Praise for *A Sabbatical in Leipzig*

'Adrian Duncan writes with emotional accuracy and
what seems like effortless precision about work and
exile, about buildings and cities. To his narratives,
he brings a mixture of the exact and the visionary.
To his characters, he brings a rawness of feeling
combined with an urgent need for them to make
sense of the world. Duncan's novels *Love Notes from a
German Building Site* and *A Sabbatical in Leipzig*, and
his collection of stories *Midfield Dynamo*, make clear
that he is an original voice, a writer who has come to
recreate the world on his own terms'
Colm Tóibín

'Adrian Duncan is one of the most interesting Irish
writers at work today. Those who have read his
novels, *Love Notes from a German Building Site* and
A Sabbatical in Leipzig, will remember the peculiar
way his protagonists see the world and the unusual
shapes his narratives take as a result. It is as if the
text is teaching you how to read anew'
Niamh Donnelly, *Irish Independent*

'At the very forefront of writing in Ireland'
Michael Cronin, *Irish Times*

'To channel the human condition through the
worldview of an engineer in this effortless but
immensely technical way is highly unusual
in fiction, especially in an era of Anglophone
interconnectedness and the drift of literature
towards a reparative or ameliorative function
which must be obvious and accessible to achieve
both market reach and wide-ranging relevance.
A Sabbatical in Leipzig is not trying to be this kind
of book. It's not trying not to be this kind of book
either, but its plain-spoken, obsessive commitment
to life as an engineering project which is not just a
cute or enabling metaphor but a dull thing of plans,
measurements, physics, accuracy and functionality
makes no attempt to bring the reader into a blunt-
edged or humanist vision of engineer-as-symbol. It's
far, far more intelligent than that. The thing is, the
engineer is a symbol, and his view of the world is
deeply, compassionately human – you just have to
earn this realisation because *A Sabbatical in Leipzig* is
not interested in spelling it out'
Niamh Campbell, *Los Angeles Review of Books*

'What's beautiful about Duncan's writing is that he
doesn't use sentimentality to tug on the heartstrings
of the reader … Michael's matter-of-fact manner
of speaking is unintentionally humorous in many
places – reminiscent of a sort of Eleanor Oliphant
character in the way he describes life events with
the tone of a bemused outsider'
Nicola Spendlove, *Crossways Literary Magazine*

'*A Sabbatical in Leipzig* is a masterclass in … paying attention to the minutest of details and looking at the world with keen eyes and a quiet but curious mind. What I enjoyed so much about this beautiful, pensive book is how it made me look at the world differently. I love the way he writes about angles and intersections, about tracing paper and shadow images, about bubbles and porcelain in such precise, luminous prose, in sentences filled with images that take your breath away. An unusual gem of a book'
Justine Carbery, *Sunday Independent*

'Despite (or, indeed, because of) the narrative style's starkness in imagery and prioritising of analysis over emotion, *A Sabbatical in Leipzig* is both haunting and devastating'
Anna Benn, *Dublin Review of Books*

A
SABBATICAL
IN
LEIPZIG

A
SABBATICAL
IN
LEIPZIG

ADRIAN DUNCAN

TUSKAR ROCK PRESS

First published in Great Britain in 2022 by
Tuskar Rock Press,
an imprint of Profile Books Ltd
29 Cloth Fair
London
EC1A 7JQ
www.serpentstail.com

First published in Ireland in 2020 by The Lilliput Press

This is a work of fiction. All characters, businesses, organizations
and events portrayed in this novel are either products of
the author's imagination or are used fictitiously.

All drawings that appear interspersed throughout the
main body of the text are by the author.

Set in 12.5 pt on 18.2 pt Kis by Marsha Swan

1 3 5 7 9 10 8 6 4 2

Printed and bound in Great Britain by
CPI Group (UK) Ltd, Croydon CR0 4YY

A CIP catalogue record for this book is available from the British Library.

ISBN 978 1 78816 970 7
eISBN 978 1 78283 941 5

To my father, Adrian

This figure shows a circle which rolls along the arc PAB for one complete revolution. Also shown is the initial position of a point P on the circle.

During the rolling of the circle, the point P is unwound as an involute of the circle from P to C in a clockwise direction.

Draw the locus of P for the combined movement.

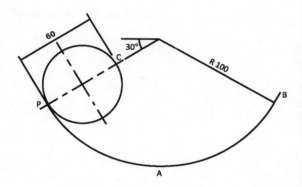

—1995 Irish Leaving Certificate Technical Drawing Examination Higher Paper 1, Question 5

[T]he more I attend to the effect produced by my words when I utter them before these bodies, the more it seems they are understood, and the words they utter correspond so perfectly to the sense of my words that there is no reason to doubt that a soul produces in them what my soul produces in me.

—Géraud de Cordemoy

PROLOGUE, FROM A PARALLEL PLACE

IN THE MORNING when I wake in the warmth beside her, our arms criss-crossing each other, connecting and sliding at points, I remember different steel suspension bridges I designed as a younger man. As we shift and we re-attach, I often visualize particularly small connections I invented, inspected, signed off, then, some time later, revisited and instructed to be repainted, repaired or replaced.

One morning, lying next to Catherine, I recalled a connection I designed many decades before to the underside of an enormous bridge that arced across the mouth of a tidal river in an isolated place in northern India, and, as she squeezed my forearm and her foot rubbed against my shin, I realized I'd miscalculated the moments and stresses that my connection was required to transmit. I bolted from the bed, envisioning collapse and disaster. I rang an office in Delhi I often had dealings with and insisted – standing in my underwear in the warm plant-lined hallway of my apartment – that I speak to an old colleague, who, when she came to the phone, told me she was surprised and pleased to hear from me again. She said I need not be alarmed because the bridge in question had been replaced three years before, after it had been all but swept away one night by a storm. Was anyone killed? I asked. No, she answered. Were we at fault? I asked. No, she replied – it was a one-in-two-hundred-year weather event.

I replaced the handset, steadied my breathing and went to the kitchen to brew a coffee. I brought a cup for Catherine too.

I returned to bed and we re-embraced differently. I lay there waiting for the sun to come up a little further before I took a sip from my cup.

I fell into a deep sleep towards which I seemed to draw Catherine too, and we didn't move again until later, far later than we had hoped, and we missed the peaceful Semana Santa parade that passes under our balcony every year, and this left us sombre and regretful for the rest of the day.

A
SABBATICAL
IN
LEIPZIG

I'VE BEEN WAKING EARLY these last few days. The mornings here in Bilbao are airy and light, and I find myself rising well before six and standing in the kitchen of my apartment, looking out the window and into the courtyard below.

My window faces west, and sometimes at this hour the morning light reflects off one of the east-facing windows a few storeys further up on the building across the courtyard from me. The light is not so strong that I can't look into it; I can look into it for a few moments longer than if I were attempting to look directly into the sun. I sometimes think, if I could arrange the windows on the east-facing façade and the corresponding windows that share my west-facing façade in such a way that for a few moments each morning I could re-direct the sun a couple of times over and back across the courtyard and into my window, then, while standing here in my kitchen, I could peer into the light for a few moments longer.

The delicacy of this arrangement of angles would mean that the sun's alignment with them would be more fleeting than if I were relying on just one window to redirect the sun towards me. The windows receiving light from each other in this way would slide more quickly out of their coalescence, but I believe the closer this complicated arrangement of windows would bring the chances of me seeing the light, and the length of time I might witness this light, to zero, then, I believe, the more beautiful I would consider this light – light I consider to be already quite lovely. I don't know my neighbours, but I am sure if I asked them they might collaborate with me and we could achieve the various angles of incidence required for me to stand for those few moments longer in my kitchen looking into the rising sun. If my neighbours on both the west and east side of the courtyard agreed on this arrangement of windows, and all of us were agreed to rise at the appointed time on a clear morning to witness our lines-of-light experiment, we could then convene down in the courtyard after the sun had disappeared and listen to how each person's experience of this light had made them feel. Their responses, though, would surely only suggest to me further questions. I then would find myself considering the quality of the glass in each person's kitchen window. I would ask myself: Were some windows double-glazed? Some single-glazed? Some recently replaced? Recently cleaned, both inside and out? What might the iron content in the glass be? How was each pane of glass cast? And what were the conditions of the casting and cooling? How might all of these factors have affected the zig-zagging channel of light over and back across our courtyard? And what sorts of losses might have occurred in this transmission? But more so, I might then learn something about my neighbours' characters by virtue of the care they show to and the knowledge they have of their kitchen windows.

A few instances ago I took up the same spot I'd assumed the last few mornings at this time, but the window across the way that usually reflects the whitened sunlight into my eyes was itself not hosting the sun. It sat instead on the edge of some unearthly luminescence. I stepped a couple of feet to my left and the reflected sun slid into view. Last night was warm and I realized this neighbour across the way must have wedged open their kitchen window to allow cooler air to circulate through their apartment as they slept.

Then, a few leaves belonging to the expansive chestnut tree in our courtyard bobbed down into view, interrupting the light reflecting off my neighbour's window, and this protected my eyes from the pain of slight overexposure I usually feel when I look for too long directly into the reflected light. The shadows of these bobbing leaves were being cast onto the dust on the outer face of my windowpane. I looked at the shadows a while as the bright flicker of the sun in the near and not-so-near distance came and went. I could not tell if I was looking at the movement of these many phenomena landing onto the dusty glass or if I was looking at the stillness of the sheet of glass itself as it partly received and admitted this movement.

This morning I woke suddenly with a pain in my knee. This happens often when I sleep on my stomach. I rolled onto my back to relieve the pain, and as I lay there a flow of mental particles depicting elements of buildings from my past appeared before me. After some time I decided that it is high time for these constructions of mine to be compiled and surveyed. I am too old, though, to do this survey. I cannot travel to these places, and if I could, I would not be able to access the nooks and crannies of each building and bridge I would need to access to carry out a survey thorough enough to ease my worries. As this thought unspooled, the name of the last place I lived in, the city of Leipzig, came to mind, especially the dot over the letter 'i' near the centre of the word, and either I moved towards it or it expanded concentrically towards me, until it filled my field of vision. Then, realizing the pain in my knee was unlikely to abate, I rose.

During the last few years of my career I mentored a young Danish engineer. I think of him often in the morning before I have my coffee and while I comb my hair. I think of the exemplary way that he could see. I do not know if he is alive or where he is now or what he might look like, but I am sure he is the only person I would trust with carrying out a survey of this kind for me.

I take a sip from my coffee and look back out the kitchen window. I can see the whole courtyard darken menacingly, then brighten again. A bird flies overhead. Its shadow runs up the rippling tree like a small dark animal fleeing the ground.

YESTERDAY I RECEIVED delivery of a second record player, a second amp and a second set of speakers I'd bought by postal order some weeks previously. Each morning, after a coffee and before I spend time honing my German-to-English translation of a set of short stories I've owned for years and that were written by a Robert Walser, I sit and listen to some Schubert. I am no expert of classical music; I barely ever listen to music – outside of the two records I own of Schubert's work. And from these records I have only ever listened closely to the first movement of his *Trout Quintet* played *allegro vivace*. I first heard this piece of music when I was a young boy working as a clerk in my father's office on the main street of my medium-sized hometown, B——, in the Midlands of Ireland. My father was a salt and turf merchant, and before I decided that engineering would be a suitable course of study I spent the winters of my mid- to late-teens working in my father's office under the tutelage of the senior clerk, Gerald, a man with a short moustache he dyed the same jet-black as the thick wiry hair that sprouted from his head. Gerald smoked often and played the transistor in his office quietly. One day, when I called into his office to run a certain set of numbers for a certain account past him, I heard the last few bars of what I learned a few moments later from the radio presenter's soothing voice was the first movement of Schubert's *Trout Quintet* played *allegro vivace*. *Franz Schubert's first movement of the* Trout Quintet *there, played* allegro vivace. But by the time I left the office, having received instruction from Gerald on

8

how to finish out my work, I had forgotten about the feeling from when I first entered the office, the feeling that insisted I find this piece of music by this Schubert and play it in its entirety to myself some day. It was not until a number of years later – on the day after we buried my mother, and we, my younger brother and my three older sisters, were gathered in the sitting room of our home in the second floor of our three-storey townhouse and my father, a few rooms over, played a record of classical music – that I thought again of this Schubert. It was not the first movement of Schubert's *Trout Quintet* my father played that time, but whatever the music was it reminded me of that moment years before when I entered Gerald's office, it directly below where my siblings and I were then sitting. Despite, on the day after my mother's funeral, being reminded of this piece of music by Schubert, I didn't act upon it until another day over two decades later when Catherine found this piece of music in a record shop called da Capo, a narrow ground-floor property halfway down Sternwartenstrasse in central Leipzig. Da Capo was the sort of shop where a person could potter around for hours undisturbed listening to records while sipping a beer or smoking a cigarette. Neither Catherine nor I smoked or drank, but we would potter around for hours in this new city, in this new, to us, record shop, looking at the various vinyls, second-hand and unused. It was here during our first week in Leipzig that we came upon this album of Schubert's work. I still listen to it each morning before I get on with my day. It's one of those handsome East-German Eterna Edition records from the early 1970s with a white sleeve. This one holds an image of a snow-covered mountaintop with conifer trees dotted in amidst swirls of eddying sleet, a reproduction of a painting by a Casper David Friedrich called *Morgennebel im Gebirge* (*Morning Mist in the Mountains*). It is an album of experimental symphonies, expanded versions of the music known as the *Trout Quintet* – and the first movement played *allegro vivace*, listed on side A, was the track I had been long seeking.

Some years after finding the first record, I came upon my second, again on a quiet Saturday evening with Catherine, sifting through the inclined planes of records organized in dense rows of elevated timber boxes to the rear of da Capo. It was also the *Trout Quintet*, but in this case played by a traditional quintet: Walter Olbertz (piano), Karl Suske (violin), Karl-Heinz Dommus (viola), Matthias Pfaender (cello) and Walter Klier (double bass), with the first movement in *allegro vivace* again listed on side A. I fell into the habit soon after of sitting in our spacious and bright living room in Leipzig, playing one version of the first movement after the other – the experimental symphony first, then the quintet: symphony, quintet, symphony, quintet, symphony. What I enjoyed most was that the melody in both sounded at the same time similar and different, and the difference I enjoyed most was that I could discern the elements of the quintet version with a clarity that satisfied me to the point of almost replacing the pleasure I had taken minutes previously from the surging experimental symphony. Not only could I visualize each musical element of the melody being generated by the quintet, but I could also discern the sliding, complicated, explicit interconnecting and releasing that went on between each instrument, and I began my imaginings then of the five East-German musicians who comprised this quintet. Even these days in Bilbao, as I listen, I often still visualize the musicians placed in a V, stemming out either side of a black centrally placed grand piano – an arrangement that is: viola, violin, piano, cello, double bass. I rarely see any distinctive features in these musicians other than their sawing and plucking and gliding hands, but more recently I picture the cellist, Pfaender, towards the middle of the arrangement, he a thin man with a mass of greying locks bouncing on his head each time he straightens from his otherwise pensive crouch around his instrument, and I see too those mere phantoms around him

11

involved in hidden acknowledgments of each other. Pfaender seems to stand apart, though, almost as if he is soon to leave the quintet.

One morning a few months back it occurred to me, while I was refitting the slim rubber belt connecting the turntable of my record player to the motor inside, that I should play both pieces of music simultaneously on two separate record players. They are two pieces of music I love unevenly, like a daughter (quintet) and a stepson (experimental symphony); they are two pieces of music that when I hear them separately I still think sometimes of my brother seated and crying quietly in my father's living room on the morning after my mother's burial, as my father put a needle to a record of, to me, unknown music in a dusty room a corridor away on the first floor of his townhouse on the main street of our busy but composed medium-sized Midlands town. When I first listened to these records, in the spacious apartment Catherine and I shared in Leipzig, I used then only to think back to Gerald and his smoke-filled clerk's office, but over time this memory has morphed and risen up one floor into my father's sitting room, where my brother still quietly cries, his arms across his chest, his dark hair dishevelled – and he sunken into my father's armchair, his shoulders bobbing.

My hope is, in playing both records simultaneously in my sitting room today, to push these images up a further storey of my father's townhouse into what was once a bedroom with a single window, which the three youngest of our family – my brother, Allen, my sister Louise and I – used to peer out of when we were children.

I PUT MY COFFEE CUP and saucer down on the table. I rub my knee. It's trembling under my weight. Some dust has swirled down from the roofs above and disappeared onto the leaves of the chestnut tree.

When I sleep on my stomach, and if my toes do not fall down over the end of the bed, the twist in my foot passes up into my body and over the hours of sleep this torsion leads to a great stiffness in my hips and knees. I sometimes think that sleep does me more harm than good.

I shift my weight and take one more sip from my coffee. I see in the courtyard below a young woman wearing a red bicycle helmet. She unlocks her bicycle from a timber railing; the chain swings to and fro as she drops it into her deep wicker basket. She checks her phone, then rolls her bicycle away. Across the top of the building opposite sweeps the shadow belonging to a tower crane I noticed yesterday evening being erected at the top of my street – the steep and narrow Solokoetxe. The shadow of the boom of the crane slides to a halt halfway up the roof across the way and the shadow of something square appears, in the process of being lowered. The sharp scent of seared bitumen and roof-felt passes and I breathe it in.

IN MY LATE TEENS, while I was studying to become a civil engineer in Dublin, I would be asked during my summer break to come home and help out with my father's salt- and turf-merchant business and particularly to assist with the turf, which usually, the first few days after I sat my end-of-year exams, would have begun to dry out on the land and be near ready for turning. Each summer I resented my being returned to this mud. I was not then, nor have never been afraid of work of a physical or mental kind, but there was something in the suddenness of returning from the world of Newtonian mechanics I'd immersed myself in throughout the previous term that sat poorly with me, and for a few days after I would have cut a sullen figure cycling up to then trudging along the borders of the boglands – me on my way to work with my father's employees in hand-extracting turf from a deep if narrow seam of what would have appeared to the untrained eye as a mere sliver of domestic bog.

I own one family-related photograph; it is a black-and-white thing and was taken by my brother, Allen, on what was to become my last day of work on my father's strip of bog on a late September afternoon in the early Sixties. I was soon to return to Dublin and complete my final year of study. The photo is taken from a slight height and it shows me second from right in a row of four other workmen all about twice my age. We are leaning on the timber handles of our tools. Extending off into the background are black-brown plains of bog. The men are wearing caps and shirts and ties. I am not wearing a cap or a tie, but the top button of my shirt is closed. We are all smiling and it would seem to me that our shift is all but done. I am sure Allen had his reasons for wanting to capture this moment, and there are six motivations I've speculated on for a while now:

—He knew I would not return to the bog
to work in this way again, and he, out of an
anticipated feeling of nostalgia, wanted to
document this place where I had spent so
many of my summers.

—He would have wanted the photograph to
perform as ballast against a type of intellectual
high falutin' in me that he at the time, I guess,
did not approve of. He was a creative person

15

but not academically bent, and he would have liked this photograph to have acted as something that tied me back to the land and work of this kind. (My suspicions for this come from him having developed three copies of this picture, one for him, one for my father and one for me – each photo creating a triangular kite of interconnection, and from each point extends further lines that converge, I imagine, on my back.)

—He wanted this photograph to remind me of him.

—This photo was simply one of the many other hundred or so he took at this time before this part of the boglands of Ireland was fully industrialized.

—He wanted this photograph to still me so that it might remind him of a version of me that he was somehow able to intuit as his favourite version of me, a person who was about to leave this part of the world, a person who would be changed by the wider world in ways that my brother foresaw and did not find to his satisfaction.

—He wanted to photograph me with these men my father employed for the wholes of

16

their lives and by doing so explain to me that I would always be somehow under my father's employ.

I think the last one is what I feel closest to now, and I believe this motivation as most likely to have inhabited something of my brother's artistic intention.

In a crowded café on Dame Street in Dublin in late October of that year, Allen, having skipped a day of school, presented me with my copy of this photograph. I thanked him, and then, not knowing quite how further to respond, asked him how his studies were going. He sipped his tea and shook his head.

THE PHOTOGRAPH IS eight by ten inches, two sizes above an average holiday snap. At my desk in my bedroom in my bedsit in Ranelagh, while completing my studies, if I found myself poring over an especially turgid problem in statics, I'd often, for respite, look up to the part of the wall upon which I had pinned the picture and take in its contents. In the evenings I'd take the picture down from the wall and imagine structures of different kinds emerging from the boglands behind – giant constructions in a variety of styles and shapes and scales. I had cheap lithographic reproductions made of this image, and in the evenings

I would draw into the distance of these reproductions the outline of further large buildings and various pieces of infrastructure – pylons, poles, transformers, chimneys, towers. The boglands stretching off into the background would become cluttered with tramlines and housing developments, and in the far distance I drew the outline of a power station with two tall chimneys and a cluster of substations positioned around its foothills, they quietly modulating the peat-generated electricity I was redirecting back out across the land and into its various townscapes, feeding homes and businesses with a flow of energy and light. Oftentimes, in my bedsit, when the evening grew late I would imagine, in one of the rooms of a house tucked away in the corner of one of my sprawling but well-laid-out bogland housing developments, a young boy crouched at his desk, with a lamp bent over his shoulder, drawing the misshapen form of a beetroot he'd happened upon earlier in the day – a beetroot which, during the high winds that whipped these landscapes the evening before, had been zapped by one of my power lines that had come loose and flailed down onto the soil below. I would then visualize this bloated beetroot growing and growing on the boy's page as he swirled his purple and green pencils outward, and this form would eventually fill my field of vision to the point of near distress and I'd detach myself by looking back to my own tiny face in the foreground of the copy of the photograph I was drawing my schematics upon, me smiling cryptically at my brother capturing the empty boglands behind the four slim workmen and me, all of us leaning on our slanes.

I have long mislaid these worked-upon and drawn-over reproductions of my brother's photograph. My hunch is I threw them out once I parsed myself of the books and lecture papers I'd collected during my studies in Dublin, around the time I moved to London to work. I still have the original photograph. I am looking at it now. It is in a delicate aluminium frame, hanging on my kitchen wall to the right of the window. I often remove the picture from the wall. In recent years I find myself doing this with increasing frequency; I slide the photograph out of its aluminium-and-glass casing and rest it on my desk in my sitting room. One at time I then place A4 sheets of acetate over the image, onto which I draw with pen and ruler a variety of designs and shapes. These designs are less involved than those I indulged in on the evenings of my final year of study back in Dublin. Now I draw mere dots, arcs, polygons and triangles that float arbitrarily above the boglands in the background of the image, as if in doing so I am somehow besting my brother – as if, in doing so, I have finally brought the abstract thoughts and new geometries I'd learned while studying in Dublin back to dangle over the bogs that Allen, it seems, was so keen for me not to forget. I have hundreds of these acetate sheets. I keep them in a box I made with glued-together plates of untreated birch ply. Some evenings I take these sheets out and place twenty of them at a time upon my brother's photograph and then slowly remove each layer until the image re-appears. Then I shuffle the twenty layers of drawings of black dots and arcs and polygons, place them over the image again and remove the layers once more, over and over, until I have vented whatever it is that urges me to undertake so repetitive an act in the first place. This oftentimes leaves me tired, and I oftentimes take myself almost immediately to bed and I oftentimes dream of near nothing, as if these simple lines and shapes and dots push from me the strange sense of dread that my usual catastrophic dreams of mishandled building materials from my past produce.

THE SUN HAS NOW LEFT the orbit of the window opposite and is inching up over the layers of glowing ivy sprawled in a rough diagonal gash across the east-facing façade. Where the ivy is thick and where it partly obscures some of the rectangular windows, the glazing behind appears, in a certain light, like dark-blue pools sunken into a vertical plain of dense and alien pasture. In the summer this ivy extends its terrain by a metre or so in each direction, then by autumn this top quadrant of the wall breaks out into a multitude of orange, yellow and pale-green dabs clinging to a light-brown and somewhat hairy sub-structure below, which in turn clings to the spalling cement covering the wall. In winter all that remains is this network of light-brown root lines of varying moisture and thickness. When I was a young boy my mother gave me the job each spring of snipping and sawing back the ivy that clung to the rear and front of our house. My mother was an anxious sort. I think now she most likely suffered from OCD. She fixated on things. The youngest four of us were given separate jobs to do at different times of the day or week or month or year, each job a tentacle of my mother's anxieties that instead of becoming sated as we worked merely grew in substance and range. My brother was asked to clean the attic on the first Tuesday evening of each month; and on the first Tuesday of each month my brother from the age of about seven would disappear up into the attic through a square in the ceiling of the hallway outside our bedroom with a candle, a paper bag and a duster and cloth in his hands. And an hour later my mother would clamber up the stepladder, lift her tiny body up into the space and I could hear them above in muffled conclave, inspecting his work. My sister Louise, a stout dark-haired girl, was asked each fortnight to ensure the hinges on every door were oiled and in good repair. She was an intelligent and systematic sort, and would produce a drawing of each floor, indicating the position of each door, and she would report to my mother on the condition of each hinge. My mother was of German stock and I think she inherited this bizarre obsession with well-installed doors from her parents. I reckon a part of every German *Zimmerei* believes that when his or her soul leaves this life what they can best leave behind is a multitude of functioning objects – particularly well-installed doors that quietly whoosh air through the spaces these doors help to carve out. My next-eldest sister was Edel. She was a frail blonde girl that I did not get on with during my childhood and with whom I had only the merest contact throughout our adult lives. She was given the job of cleaning the windows of the house every fourth day, with a cloth, soapy water and day-old copies of the *Irish Times*. Her job was arduous and I think it created a sense of injustice in her, which may have also contributed to the distance between us. She'd often ask my mother why Allen and I had been given such infrequent and light work, whereas she was lumbered with cleaning the stiff old sash windows to the front and rear of each storey of our house. Edel would often complain to my mother, asking her if we could swap jobs, and my mother would just stare at her, as if the crossing of lines of our labour in this way was a suggestion emanating from the depths of some kind of madness. My eldest sister, Jo, who was four years older than Edel, avoided these chores because she was already in her late teens by the time my mother's obsessions began appearing. All of this might suggest my mother did nothing to contribute to the upkeep of the house. Quite the opposite; she did everything else, and had she been less rigid in how she busied us all she could easily have asked us for help and lessened her burdens. My father took almost no part in any of this, he being out for most of each day attending to the many parts of his successful salt- and seasonal-turf business.

Each spring, my work involved climbing up onto a stepladder and snipping or sawing back the ivy branches that had grown too unruly for my mother. Her concern was that if the ivy spread too far it would then take root too deeply into the walls of our home and perhaps damage the brickwork and draw dampness into the interior of our otherwise dry and warm abode. As such, the ivy on our house, through the years up until my mother died, when I was seventeen, was always cut back in a neat horizontal fringe to the same height as the lintels of our ground-floor windows of which there were four that fronted onto the main street, two each side of my father's office entrance – a broad, blue timber-panelled door of frosted glass with the words 'Pura Salt' arcing in slim golden capitals across the upper third of the main pane. I see our house now covered over utterly in this ivy, like a tiny block in the palm of a giant green-fingered hand, and the ivy now pushing through the roof slates, dislodging them slowly; and every now and then I see a slate falling, crashing to the ground, slate after slate, I imagine, until some ghost-like delegates from the local council visit, deem the structure to be unsafe and decide to take action. I imagine the local council either takes the building in hand and refurbishes it or, more likely, fits sheets of plywood to the windows and doors and then surrounds the building with temporary fencing upon which council labourers affix signs demarcating the place as a hazardous ruin, with entry at the risk of those who enter.

MY THROAT TIGHTENS for a moment. I cough. And cough again. I pull a tissue from my pocket and rub my mouth with it, then ball the tissue up and throw it onto the kitchen table. As it tumbles into the light its whiteness shimmers, and I realize this crumpled ball of paper is also about the size and shape of a small animal's brain.

UNTIL I MET CATHERINE, I spent most of my life trying to shed objects from which I felt I had extracted my use. Then, over the forty years or so we spent together as boyfriend and girlfriend, I began to accumulate things again. Once or twice a year, outside of necessities, I might have bought a book or a new set of pencils, and once or twice, while out walking the streets of Leipzig, Catherine and I might have happened upon a pleasing item of furniture. Catherine was by no means a hoarder, but she had an easier relationship with useless objects than I. Over the last six years, since she's been gone, I've slipped back into the habit of ridding myself of objects again. This second record player, this second amp and this second set of speakers are the first objects of leisure I have bought since a day about a dozen years ago when I purchased, as a gift for Catherine, an old DDR-era Praktica camera from a second-hand shop in central

Leipzig, two streets away from Catherine's then place of work, the Grassi Museum of Applied Arts, where she was employed as a researcher and exhibition designer. The only other gift I bought Catherine was a set of table-tennis bats I found in the same shop a good number of years before I bought the camera. These bats sit in a bag in my bedroom. The bag, a well-used, spacious but by now musty thing of leather and felt, lies under my shirts in the second drawer of my bedroom dresser. Sometimes I take the bats out of the bag and handle them. Inside the bag lies her old leather wallet with some dollar coins, some folded-up euros, a few old East-German ten-mark notes and a passport photo of her as a young woman. In the back compartment of the bag there's a large envelope filled with all of the Post-it Notes and lists and messages scribbled on slips of paper that we left for each other, usually on the kitchen table of our apartment, when we lived together in Leipzig. She collected these things for years without my knowing. I found the envelope in the back of her bedside locker one day when I was clearing out our apartment before I moved here to Bilbao. When I peered into the envelope that morning I could tell what she had done, and I sealed the envelope over. I did not then, and do not now consider these things as my possessions.

The last piece of advice she gave me before she became very ill and went under with morphine was that I should do stretches every morning. She said it was important I remain limber because if I were to become old and immobile then there would be no one there to help me move.

Every morning, after I have a coffee, listen to Schubert, try to read these short stories by Walser, but before I leave to visit a set of enormous steel sculptures, made by an artist called Richard Serra, on display in the nearby Guggenheim Museum, I turn the chair at my desk in my sitting room into the room and do some stretches. Later this morning I will sit and reach my arms above me for ten seconds, then I will reach my arms out before me, then bend forward and try to reach my outstretched feet. I will do this three times down the middle of my body, then I will lean my body to the right and do it once, then lean my body to the left and do it once again. I will then stand at a wall in the sitting room and lay my palm flat against it at shoulder height, step forward and stretch out my shoulder tendons and the muscle that connects my shoulder to my chest bone. I will do this to the other shoulder, then over and back thrice again.

FOR THE FIRST FEW YEARS in Leipzig I was on a sabbatical from work, or, it was more like gardening leave that turned into an extended career break. For the fifteen years previous I'd worked as a design engineer for a large engineering consultancy on a number of what might be called prestigious buildings in the UK and France. The job that forced me into taking this sabbatical had been cancelled mid-construction on account of a range of huge cracks that appeared one night in the basement of the building. Through these cracks poured gallons of foul water from dozens of sources. The geotechnical survey had miscalculated the depth to the bedrock beneath the site and we, the structural engineers on the job, had designed foundations – a forty-by-fifty-metre grid of thirty-metre-long concrete tubes – that were not suitable to the conditions beneath the surface. The bedrock these stilt-like tubes were supposed to bear onto was on average thirty-two metres below the surface of the ground and our tubes fell two metres short throughout. We were building a new library and civic centre for a small town in rural France, the funding for which had been raised through local lotteries and government grants. After this disaster our company was criticized in the newspapers for weeks on end. Then came a drawn-out legal row over who should shoulder the blame for the faulty foundation design. We accused the geotechnicians; they of course accused us for not responding with enough diligence to one of the clauses in their design, which stated that all recommendations they made should be checked in actuality by us before construction began. We won the case on the basis of this absurd clause, but it cost us greatly and it put the geotechnics company out of business. Some weeks later the principal of the geo-technics company, an old colleague of mine from my first few years in London and of whom I was par-ticularly fond, was found dead from an overdose of sleeping pills and vodka. He left behind him a wife and two children. I think often of those two metres of black boulder clay between the tips of our tubes and the surface of the bedrock sufficient in stiffness to receive them. I think often of the tips of the tubes sinking like pencils into dough, and the settlement forces this transferred back up to the metre-thick basement slab of this library – forces large enough to bring about these massive cracks and to allow this foul water to emerge and spill across the surface of the basement. I can still recall the smell of faeces and creosote that night we were called to site, all of us barely breathing with shock.

During these court cases Catherine moved to take up this position at the Grassi Museum in Leipzig. Our relationship was disintegrating on account of these nasty vectors pulling at my psyche and in turn tugging at hers. So, one afternoon a few weeks after the disagreement was settled and a few days after I heard of my old colleague's demise, I called Catherine from the south terminal in Heathrow airport telling her I had cleared my apartment in central London, left the consultancy, emptied my bank account and was in a phone booth near the departure gates with a ticket in my hand for Berlin, and I asked her if she would like me to be with her. I don't know if you can hear someone smile on the phone, but I am sure she smiled as she said, "Please, dear Michael, do please come."

PORCELAIN IS THE MATERIAL I associate most with Catherine. I have kept one porcelain cup and saucer of hers. I use it every second day. I'm using it today. The other cup I use is a plain shallow pewter thing I bought here in Bilbao. It holds a mouthful or two of coffee. The porcelain cup was given to Catherine as a gift from the Grassi Museum on the occasion of her last day of work. She was overwhelmed when she received it. The museum had undergone a renovation and re-build during the last half-decade or so of Catherine's time there, and she was centrally involved in how the applied-arts exhibition was designed, especially the section of the exhibit used for the display of porcelain. She had traveled regularly over the years to and from Dresden, where she visited the porcelain collection in the Zwinger Palace. She often told me that she could learn from the Zwinger Palace collection how to mishandle an exhibition design; she said the great flaw of the Zwinger Palace exhibition design at this time was that it ended with a collection of figurines from the late 1700s, they all of Germanic style, illustrating the supposed baroque heights the material had risen to in its European manifestation, but then, in the Zwinger Palace, the viewer was re-routed back through the exhibition, back through the fascinating kitchenware of the mid-1700s, back through Augustus the Strong's life-like animal figures and, fatally, back through the Chinese and Japanese porcelain of the 1400 to 1600s, from which all of this emerged. Catherine always said it was in this last part of the walk, back through the Far-Eastern origins of the material (delicately painted and coated pots, vases, plates) so soon after witnessing the porcelain of the late 1700s, that the vulgarity of the European work in this material became suddenly apparent. So, Catherine insisted that the porcelain exhibition in her beloved Grassi in Leipzig would be modest and would lead the visitor through the material's development chronologically and in one direction only, to 'protect the Germans from ridicule', she said. Her other contribution to this part of the exhibition was a wall she designed at the end of the exhibit upon which were placed, on tiny glass shelves, ninety-five porcelain cups and saucers from the 1740s to early 1800s, all made by manufacturers in northern France, Austria and Germany, 'a living cross-section', she called it, of the designs and styles in porcelain of this kind then available in Europe. An unusually observant visitor looking at this wall today might notice that there are only ninety-four cups in place; there is a gap in the bottom left-hand corner of the display – and this was why Catherine was so overwhelmed on receiving this gift, because her colleagues had given this last cup and saucer to her as a parting gesture for her work on the museum over those difficult years of re-establishment they had all endured together. I remember Catherine's hands covering her small mouth when her colleagues unveiled this gift on the night of her retirement party, because she knew it was one of the few cups and saucers made by the arcanist Stöltzel, of whom she had developed curiosity and admiration. I remember Catherine when we got home that night crying with pride in her work and with the joy she felt from receiving this cup and saucer. Then one afternoon a few weeks later I walked into the sitting room and she was looking out onto Prager Strasse, her arm across her stomach. She turned to me and I could see that her eyes were wet. I asked her why she was upset and she said that she had been thinking of work and that she was ashamed of the jealousy she felt towards the working conditions she had helped leave behind in the redeveloped Grassi, 'settled working conditions', she said in her clipped Geordie accent – conditions that she said she would have loved to have experienced in her own professional time there.

When I first met Catherine she was completing a doctorate in applied arts, specializing in Chinese-style porcelain production in Dresden during the 1700s – the years of the 'white gold of Saxony', as she once told me. I knew of porcelain then more so as the material used as the nodes on the top of the electricity poles, where the wires carrying the electricity are connected. Porcelain is considered a sort of magic insulating substance in the world of electrical engineering. When I was a teenage boy I remember a Rural Electrification Scheme linesman sitting astride a newly installed pole along the outer edges of my hometown, and screwing one of these skull-sized nodes of porcelain into position onto the upper arm at the top the pole. I remember looking on for an age, one bright afternoon, at this single technician hanging from a fabric harness slung around the tip of the pole; I could sense the great weight and density of the smooth white porcelain object in his hand. It was not until years later, while out walking among a row of new poles and pylons, installed a few miles south west of my father's sliver of bogland, that I once again encountered one of these nodes lying nestled in the grass, left behind by some absent-minded electricity-supply worker. I looked for some time at the smooth, almost shiny, white porcelain object resting in this clump of grass. It occurred to me that perhaps it would be best if I did not pick it up. I thought that by leaving it unmolested I could preserve my memory of that Rural Electrification Scheme worker sitting astride the crux of the electricity pole those years before, and particularly the way his otherwise robust-looking wrist flopped back under the foreign weight of the smooth skull-sized thing. I don't know how long I stood peering down at this object, but I do know that while I did it began to rain gently. The rain fell in broken lines from over my shoulders, the drops ruffled the grass before me, splattering onto the surface of the polished porcelain node, it lying like a corpse in a long-left-uncovered grave.

I am sure I told Catherine often, during the first few times we stepped out, about my ignorance of decorative porcelain, including this lonely and tactless encounter in that field near my father's sliver of domestic bog, and I am sure she found my ignorance of decorative porcelain and my knowledge of porcelain as a material of good electrical resistance amusing.

Her cup and saucer is sitting on the kitchen table in front of me now. Its shadow extends out across the table from underneath the lip of the saucer. The rim of the cup is gold-coloured. A thick band along the upper third of the otherwise white vessel hosts a twisting pattern of oak leaves on a background of purple. The handle of the cup loops up over the rim into an elongated void with two embellished golden points of connection to the cup, one at mid-height and the other swooping down to the near underside of the bowl. Then the cup bulges out and down to a gold-edged circular base, the ridge of which sits perfectly in the saucer. The saucer is almost flat, with two concentric, centimetre-thick coloured bands, one in a purple similar to the band on the cup above it, and another in sky blue with a repeat of the twisting golden pattern of oak leaf flourishing around it. This cup and saucer is a light and pleasant thing to hold and drink from. Inside it now lies a pool of coffee, a tiny black disc obscuring its base. I down the lukewarm mouthful, lift the cup and inspect the underside. There's a tiny red mark in the shape of a shield or perhaps a beehive inscribed into the middle of the base. This glyph appears on the underside of the saucer too. Each time I replace the cup and saucer back on the shelf in our kitchen, I ensure that both sets of red inscriptions point to the wall – markings that rest not much more than a millimetre of porcelain apart.

I take a glistening prune from the small blue bowl of six on the table, chew on it a while, then drop the wet stone into the cup. I turn from the window and walk down the dimly lit corridor. It is the coolest portion of the apartment. I grow a row of six succulents – three cacti, two jade and an aloe – on a slatted timber bench placed along the wall at halfway. They don't take much to maintain, and they expand in millimetres each year. The floorboards, broad planks of darkened cedar, are creaking somewhat under my footsteps. My apartment building is a brick-wall and timber-joist structure, erected at the turn of the last century in what was once a luxurious part of the old city. This form of construction, when my neighbours come home from their work in the evenings, leads to countless shudders being passed down through the structure towards my living space. Those that live above me are a young, robust and particularly heavy-footed couple. I look up and listen. They have just put on their shoes and are stomping around between their bathroom and their front door, preparing to leave. They stop, speak to each other for a second or two, then I hear a set of keys splash to the ground, a scrape, then a door opening and closing and the pounding steps of someone outside in the communal stairwell. The other person upstairs then paces into the kitchen, pauses, paces back to the hallway once more. I imagine this person putting a bag over a shoulder, then the door opens and closes again, and a more nimble set of footsteps descends the stairwell outside, and the place falls quiet again. I walk towards the end of the corridor, past my toilet and bedroom, and enter my living room, where now sit the two sets of record players and amps and speakers. The living room leads onto a small balcony, and some nights when I am particularly restless I sit out there waiting and listening to the city and to the port in the distance too.

There are seven bridges all within a mile or so of me. They span over the Estuary of Bilbao, a broad river that winds through the city, and from my balcony at night I imagine these edifices quietly arching in the semi-dark. I visit them every day and I will see them later today too as I amble up towards the Guggenheim Museum to walk around this set of enormous steel sculptures I've come to know.

When I arrived first at this apartment I decided I would carry out a survey of the ten bridges that cross the Estuary of Bilbao. I took my old notebook, a pencil and my city map with me and documented these things – span, material, width, height, general repair. But because each day now my route only reaches the first seven, I consider the last three bridges (the Puente Pedro Arrupe, the Puente de Deuste and the Puente Euskalduna) as distant strangers. The seven I do know, I admire and disdain for different reasons, like the way one might admire or disdain friends within a group you know well.

My father was born a twin, but his brother died two months after he was born for reasons unknown to me. I think of this twin when I pass the first bridge on my route. Once, on either side of the Church of Saint Antony, at the point where the Solokoexte meets the Estuary of Bilbao, arched two bridges. On the right of the church a stone bridge called, I believe, the Puenta Marzana was first built. It once connected the broad Kalea Somera to the steep and narrow Muelle da Marzana on the other side. But the bridge was replaced 150 years ago with another, the Puente de San Antón to the east of the church. However, the two bridges stood either side of the church for a number of years before the bridge that I believe was called the Puenta Marzana was finally removed. The Puente de San Antón is a fine double-span masonry bridge whose northernmost rampart swerves around and up to the rear wall of the Church of Saint Antony. At this junction the difference in hardness between the sandstone of the church and granite of the bridge becomes apparent. The sharpness of the corners of these cut stones contrasts greatly. This is at the river side of the building, and if you look up from this junction of material the whole church, its dome, its carvings and statues look all to have somewhat melted. If you round the church to the main entrance on the busy Kalea Ribera you can see that the heads and the clothes of the apostles and saints have almost entirely wasted away, as if some plague of locusts descended on them many years ago. Whenever I enter the church, these phantasms fall away, and I can calmly take in the sandstone structure inside. Here the carvings, details and sculptures are all perfectly crisp, and I realize the difference between outside and inside is the difference between before and after rubbing sleep out of your eyes in the morning. The world inside becomes vivid and serious, so when I take in the deformed and diminished figures on the church's exterior I think often of their concerted sibling versions safe within.

One day in late January, during the first few weeks I lived on the Solokoexte and when I first began frequenting the front bench – or on cold days the front window of La Gernikesa, a small café I visit each morning – I spotted, among the schoolchildren and parents gathering at the junction of traffic lights, a host of people with pets of great variety. As the schoolchildren and parents veered left, those with their animals veered right and disappeared into the Church of Saint Antony across the road. I paid for my coffee and wandered over to see what was afoot. The whole building was full of humans and an immediate cacophony of animals and birds – barking, trilling, grunting, miaowing and panting, all attending a brief service. At the end of the service each creature was brought forward to the celebrant for blessing, and I learned later that day when I read a touristic pamphlet made available at the church that in these parts Saint Antony is not only the patron saint of lost things, but he is also the patron saint of animals.

To the right of the front entrance of the church there's a disfigured statue of a saint or some representation of a person important to the story of Saint Antony, but I have no idea who it might be. The lower half of the head has all but disintegrated and the upper half has slumped onto the chest of the figure, as if he has fallen asleep mid-invocation. My route to the Guggenheim each day takes me past this church, this statue, and down the river side of the Mercado Ribera, a fine old market that smells of fresh fish and fresh coffee. The walkway between the river and the market wall narrows here and is usually peopled by workers smoking, or students hunkered on the ground. After this the Puenta de la Ribera appears. It is a precast concrete footbridge whose two main segments curve up, in pale quarter-circles, to a midpoint, where they rest against each other and gather up into themselves an everyday sort of stillness that I almost nod to each time I pass. The middle of the bridge flattens out into a walkway that leads up over the bank on the opposite side and onto Kalea Conde Mirasol, and from there the city rises and goes out of my reach. If I were to walk up that hill I would be so tired afterwards that I would not be able to continue on to the museum, and I would certainly struggle to climb the hill back to my apartment at the end of the day. So I turn from this pleasing and simple bridge and usually take a hold of the parapet along the side of the river bank, which by then has transformed from the muscular white stone flanking the market into a slim, snow-white cast-iron railing that has been painted upon so many times over the years that the form of the metal beneath has been softened and rounded out. I run my hand along this railing as I walk, feeling for imperfections as I go. The city is quiet here, and on warm days, here is where it is also at its coolest. This is the only part of my route where I'm not distracted by the city and its many patterns and I often think of Catherine here. The bridge that follows is the Puente La Merced. It's a cast-concrete thing and is so little used that if I were mayor I would have it removed. I'm always glad when I'm past it because the city, in the following twenty paces, comes to life again and I can forget myself. This is all I want from the city: that it allow me to forget. I don't want to die in my apartment circling myself; I want to fall over here in the city, slump to the ground, expire among the shivering trees and be carried away by strangers.

Most days, I stop for a while at the Puente del Arenal. It is not that I particularly like this bridge – it is a stolid three-span cast-concrete thing, but the landscapes it connects have such exuberance that by the time I arrive at this turn in the river the whole aspect seems to cleave open above me and from this opening pour many artefacts: the Plaza Nueva, the Church of Saint Nicholas, the Arriaga Theatre and the Puenta del Arenal itself, with its shallow arcs and its eight five-lanterned lamps atop. Then to the left of this, where the preposterous façade of Bilbao's main train station yawns out over the western bank of the river, the ornate and twinkling Building of Bilbao rises up, interrupting the rectilinear high-rises clambering up the hills beyond, which then transform into trees and greenness upon a mountain that eventually ridges into a distant line.

On the south-eastern side of the bridge there is a passageway that continues onto my favourite part of the walk. It is about a hundred yards of a stroll that leads up to the beautiful Puente del Ayuntamiento and beyond to the palm-lined Paseo Campo Volatín. In these open spaces I open too. I feel like I am open to the point of being ripped asunder. Sometimes on this stretch I feel my old body made bare to every pattern I can muster. Then, as I round this passageway, the absurd, glinting Guggenheim looms into view.

)))))

I HAD A LITTLE DIFFICULTY finding my second record player, my second amp and my second set of speakers, because I wanted to replicate the models of these items of technology as best I could. It took some time tracking down the exact versions, but the record players are now both Telefunken, the amps both Onkyo and the speakers both Hena box speakers from the late 1970s. Catherine and I purchased the first set of objects from a market stall on the weekend after I first joined her in Leipzig. Both of us were buoyed at my arrival and the promise of our closeness to each other. We walked around the market holding hands on a warm day in early June. The bespectacled bric-a-brac trader on the stall where we bought the record player told Catherine, who could then already speak German well, that Telefunken had been established as an arm of the electrical company Siemens at some time during the turn of the last century. I found its name somewhat curious – *tele* the Latin for 'distant' and *funken* the German verb 'to radio'. I found it as awkward an amalgamation then as I do now, looking over and back at the two record players in the sitting room before me. I unpacked these purchases yesterday evening a few hours after they had been delivered. I first pulled my armchair alongside the record player, amp and speakers I've always had here, they arranged on a steel-and-timber table alongside the wall of my sitting room. The two record sleeves holding Schubert's music lean in the gap between the speakers on the lower shelf of the table. I unfolded and pulled another similarly sized table into position opposite my first record player, amp and speakers, and adjacent to the chair now facing the opposite wall – a wall that is almost totally bare. In this corridor-like arrangement of machines I'll listen today to the two versions of Schubert's first movement of the *Trout Quintet* in *allegro vivace*, playing simultaneously, while I sit and stare at the sitting-room wall opposite.

I lift open the lid on the new player and blow some particles of dust off the shining record. I unplug the red and black cables connecting the new player to the new amp, and the new amp to the two new speakers. Before I re-insert the cables I blow into each connector. Then I give each connection a wiggle to make certain each point is solid. I turn everything on and watch the small red power lights on the amp and record player illuminate. I tilt the arm belonging to my new record player up and reach underneath with my fingertip to touch the needle. A muffled thud crunches from the speakers. I turn everything off and stand over the machines, then I look to my desk and to the crumpled copy of Walser's short stories that lies on top of it.

AS I SIT AT MY DESK beside the window, three images close in on me. One is the image I mentioned earlier of the painting of a mountaintop shrouded in mist by Casper David Friedrich that features on the cover of my Eterna Edition version of Schubert's *Trout Quintet* re-imagined as experimental symphonies; another is a picture of the writer Robert Walser, his body lying face down in a field of snow, it a photograph from a newspaper cutting shown to me by Catherine some years ago and which I still believe to be one of the loneliest pictures I have ever seen; the third is from a postcard pinned to the wall above my desk that Catherine and I found in a flea market in London when we first began seeing each other. This postcard has a picture to the front depicting a range of mountain peaks covered over in snow and surrounded by wispy clouds. Typed upon the top third of the picture in block capitals are four names, and from each delicate arrows indicate to what mountain peak they refer: Dent D'Hérens (4,173m), Cervino (4,478m), Breithorn (4,171m), Roccia Nera (4,089m).

I am not entirely sure if this is something I remember as having happened, or if I am remembering the following from what I drew onto the cheap lithographic reproductions of my brother's photograph while I was taking a break from my undergraduate studies, or perhaps it is one of the few memories I have of my parents arguing, but I seem to recall a number of German engineers coming and going regularly from my hometown during the late 1950s, when I was perhaps twelve or thirteen years of age. 'Large-boned and good-looking and able to drink', is how I remember my mother describing them. I recall seeing a clutch of these yellow-haired men convening on a structure, about the size of a cottage, being built on the far edge of my father's sliver of domestic bog.

It was a model of a substation being installed on the land and was demolished soon afterward once the Irish engineers for the Electricity Supply Board had understood its workings. This full-scale model was built with a steel pylon beside it and with wires leading down from the pylon into the back of this flat-roofed structure. But the wires, instead of spanning out across the countryside, stopped at the pylon; they were cauterized at source, it seemed to me. They made a forlorn coupling of objects, sitting there in the middle of this field illustrating how power might be regulated elsewhere. Though the building was house-sized, it had no front door. Its walls were a beige yellow and had a row of tiny square windows running under the eaves, and underneath that, in the middle of the wall, protruded a declarative black circle with a flattened Z running through it, denoting a lightning strike or simply a crackle of electricity. One wet day when the work in the bog had been called off, I decided to walk across the land and sneak a look at the substation's workings. I swung myself over a locked gate and approached the building. The door in the left gable was open so, gingerly, I peered in and entered the dusky single-chamber structure. To my left stood a row of seven eight-foot-tall and three-foot-wide coils of most likely copper resistors. They seemed to be connected in series along the length of the wall; and from the top of each coil ran two thick wires covered over in a sort of rubber. The place smelt of oil, cement, electrics and silage. I have not encountered that combination of smells since. The room lay in darkness, but overhead small shafts of light splayed in from the line of windows placed high along the elevation, as if I were all of a sudden within a one-tenth-scale model of an unfinished gothic cathedral at daybreak. There were no controls of any kind, just these coils of oiled copper. I went back outside and turned to inspect the rear of the building to where the rubber-coated wires led. There, on a stack of poles, reclined a red-haired man of about twenty-five years who I immediately recognized as a former employee of my father's. His feet were resting up on a pole he'd rolled out in front of him and he had positioned himself under the back canopy that extended a foot or so from the roof. This man was reading what looked to be a newsletter of some kind. He peered up and immediately recognized me as the son of the person who'd once given him employment. I think he might have been one of the Kennedys or the Kinsellas, I can't be sure, but I associate him for some reason with a family of workhouse masons who had migrated east from Kildare to B——. I remember this Kennedy or Kinsella chap clearly as a playful and excitable type and he was then of course working for 'the scheme'. We chatted for a while and I asked him what he was reading, and he told me he was leafing through the *Rural Electrification Office Newsletter*, and that he'd just learned how many poles had been erected in his district during the last quarter, and how many miles of wire the rural electrification team in this district had strung and how many houses they'd connected up. He listed out a range of numbers that impressed him but that I could not possibly have fully understood. Then he asked me to sit down on the pole beside him. So I sat, and he laughed and told me I was now sitting on a little piece of Finland. I chuckled too, but out of confusion. I was unsure where Finland was. I imagined it to be a northern place and perpetually covered in snow. He told me all of the poles in this district had been shipped from Finland earlier in the year, and that we, the Irish State, had bought hundreds of thousands of trees – 'forests' worth', he said – to use as poles to hold our electricity cables aloft. He pointed to five blocky glyphs scored into the side of the creosoted poles we were sitting on and told me if the first character in this code was a letter then the tree came from Finland, and if it was a number then the pole was from Ireland; and if it was from Ireland it was probably a hardwood, and in that case the type of crampons one might use to scale the pole required sharper teeth. He then flicked further through the rather delicate-seeming booklet and showed me what looked like a script for a play, and he told me these were dispatches recorded from an ocean-going steamer travelling from a port in Helsinki to a port in Limerick in the autumn of the previous year, it laden with thousands of stripped Finnish trees. He said these dispatches had been made by radio from the ocean-going steamer to any ports on land that could receive its signal. The dispatches were terse, sometimes single-line, utterances and this red-haired young man, sitting on these Finnish trees stacked behind this German substation, began to act out the correspondences. He put his cupped hand to his mouth and made that theatrical 'krshh' sound over and over again, 'krshh, krshh, come in, krshh, come in, krshh, krshh, losing poles, krshh, krshh, swells over fifty feet, krshh', and he looked to me, pushed some strands of his dark-red hair from his forehead, and, 'krshh, vessel hove to, shipping heavy water over cargo, krshh, losing steering, krshh, shifting of deck, pump port tank, krshh, krshh, krshh, wind at hurricane strength', then he licked his lips, smiled and put his cupped hand back to his mouth, 'krshh, abandon approach, krshh, abandon approach, krshh, seeking shelter in Rosshaven, krshh, await sun up, krshh, await improving weather, proceed to Duncansby Head, krshh, wind veering to east ... .' He stood up on the pole he'd been resting his feet upon, swayed there a moment, and pretended to be a tree being felled, keeling his stiffened body over and landing on his face like a statue being toppled. He fell and stood four, five, six times; then, as he lay in the wet grass, he continued to report once more on this treacherous trip from Helsinki to Limerick Port, 'Krshh, man overboard, poles overboard, krshh, man overboard, krshh, poles overboard, crew overhauling lashings ... krshh,' and I am pretty sure I began to laugh, and as I laughed I remember conflating the mountainous swells of the sea I imagined these dispatches having emanated from with the vast forest-cleaved whites of this Arctic place called Finland, with the figure of this man lying on the ground before me, repeating, 'krshh, krshh, krshh' – and I am not sure if it is his radio signals that have brought about this mirth now, but I am laughing still in my sitting room in my apartment in the Old Town of Bilbao, visualizing this variety of images and useful instruments while looking at this postcard of snow-covered Alpine peaks pinned to the white wall before me, especially the peak with the German name Breithorn whose height above sea level is indicated as 4,171 metres, while to the left bulges upward another peak, which in actuality must be scores of miles away from the Breithorn, this one with a French name Dent D'Hérene whose height above sea level is indicated, with a small arrow hovering above it, as 4,173 metres, and I wonder at the two-metre difference between these two indications. I think back to the rear of the model substation located to the south west of my father's sliver of domestic bog and I remember why this playful young man eventually lost his job with the scheme – he was caught cutting off the bottom fifth of the poles he was trusted with thrusting into the ground. My father told me that this excitable young man had become obsessed with the performance numbers in the quarterly newsletter and wanted to outdo the other districts of the scheme in the category of 'poles erected', and this young man had reckoned that if he cut the bottom metre or two off each pole then the gang of labourers he was in charge of could dig the hole for the pole one metre or so shallower than standard, and this excitable young man must then have calculated how much this elision would save him and his gang of labourers in time and effort over the course of the many poles they were instructed to erect. I wonder now where he cast those metre-or-so lengths of Finnish timber aside: In ditches? Into the bog? A river? Or maybe he made some other use of this cast-aside timber that I cannot remember or imagine. And I wonder now what the pit of his stomach felt like the day he began noticing the poles he and his team had erected, tilting on the landscape and pulling the electrical wires they were supposed to support into somewhat sinister patterns across the sky.

I PICK UP my tiny paperback of Walser's short stories and flip through some pages. The delicate clangs of the tower crane outside drift in and I can hear the thrum of a car turning at the front corner of my building. It accelerates down towards the bridge and over the, I imagine, gushing Estuary of Bilbao. The diffracted morning light is warming up the room. I open Walser's short stories on page eight. The first ten pages of the book are crinkled, dog-eared and written over considerably. The margins are almost black with notes and counter-notes. I found this copy one weekend near the end of my five years of sabbatical in Leipzig. Catherine was away at a conference back in London on the invite of the V&A to present her research on the developments in porcelain-painting styles emerging in Dresden during the early 1700s.

After I purchased this book I called into the Museum für Bildende Kunst in the middle of Leipzig to see an exhibition of works by the Austrian landscape painter Joseph Anton Koch. The front of my Eterna Edition version containing Schubert's *Trout Quintet* as played by the five East-German musicians shows a detail of a painting by Koch. The painting was called *Der Schmadribachfall* and I was curious to see if the entire painting might feature in the show. It did, and the reproduction on my Eterna Edition record – even the detail – did the earthy colours and texture in the painting very little justice. To the foreground of the detail a broad river courses past and on the outcrop of land in the centre a man is taking aim with what looks like a rifle, he in the act of shooting at a dispersing herd of deer fleeing up through the woods to the right. In that moment, just over the ridge of this outcrop, appears the top half of another hunter, one that can be assumed from the narrative relayed by Koch to be a slower-moving sportsman than the lead character of the piece. To the left, and seemingly running in an opposite direction to the fleeing deer, scatter a pack of five hunting dogs. The man firing his rifle could barely be more centred. However, in the painting I saw that day in the gallery, the man is but a speck near the bottom edge, shrunken in scale against the sublime natural grandeur towering above him. The river that gushes from right to left across the foreground of the detail of the picture, and that takes up merely the bottom quarter of the painting in its entirety, is a section of a long river that flows down in zig-zags over many miles of idyllic landscape from the top of a distant snow-peaked mountain behind. The detail is cropped in such a way that it seems as if the viewpoint is directly from the other side of the river, almost at the same altitude as the man shooting at the deer fleeing into the woods. But in Koch's original oil painting, which is well over a metre tall, the viewpoint, which incorporates the great mountains and the heavens beyond, seems to be lifted above the height from where the cropped detail is composed, as if by some trick of the eye the viewpoint has been re-created in the painting from some more-elevated position halfway up the other side of the opposite valley. In the background of Koch's painting, he depicted, according to the reading material that accompanied the exhibition, the Breithorn range of peaks. These appear also, but from the Italian side of the range, on the front of the postcard I have pinned to my otherwise naked living-room wall.

I lift the postcard from the wall. On the rear of it I read that sometime in 1958 it was sent to a Luigi Belluco, who presumably lived then in Milan. The handwriting in the message part of the postcard is in the Italian language and its lettering is and always has been illegible to me – I cannot even make out who sent this postcard. I sometimes wonder how it ended up in that shop in London. Did this Luigi Belluco move to London and bring it with him, and when he died or when he cleared out his apartment or house was this postcard put into a box, then unearthed and brought to the second-hand shop in London where I found it? I do not think of Luigi as the type of person that would leave Milan, or, if he were to leave, it would not be for London. I feel Luigi might have died in Milan and when his belongings were boxed away and brought to a second-hand shop somewhere in the city, that an unknown visitor from London then came upon this postcard – an unknown person with similar tastes to mine, who was taken by this photographic print depicting this arrangement of snowy peaks with arbitrary names and numbers pointing delicately at them, interrupting the heavens with such useful but imprecise things as estimated heights above sea level.

I place the postcard into this book of Walser's work, between the pages that hold a story I've fixated on over the last few years. It is titled '4' and is one of six very short tales, collectively titled *Sechs Kleine Geschichte* (*Six Small Stories*), which he wrote in his twenties. '4' is a mere 211 words and it describes a writer in a darkened room looking at a wall. The writer in the short story then claims this wall to be in his *Kopf*, his head, and this writer then, after offering to swap his physiology for that of the wall's, takes flight from this wall, or equally likely, this writer projects this flight onto the bare wall while still sitting quietly and staring at it. The writer, who is also the narrator, who is also, I suppose, Walser, describes the adventure with a list of words that suggest he has magically and seamlessly flown over a landscape of 'fields, meadows, paths, forests, villages, towns, rivers', which, once brought into being through these words, are then halted by the narrator, who then laughs at these categories and places, claiming, all of a sudden, that he has gathered them back into his *Schädel*, his skull. This narrator throws open and then closes over these idyllic places – finally taking them as his own. He is generous and covetous. More recently, while I have been reading through this story the registers of meaning shift chaotically and I become confused and somewhat lost. The experience is close to what might be called 'homesickness', but because I have not felt homesick in perhaps sixty years I cannot certainly say my experience is this feeling of homesickness. To counter this feeling I am unable to name, these days I often take out the Eterna Edition record of Schubert's *Trout Quintet* as produced by the five East-German musicians and I place the sleeve of the record with its detail of Koch's painting in front of me and I imagine the painting as having been composed from the position of Walser's wall, the wall he gazed at while writing his strange and baffling '4'. Sometimes I play the music quietly in the background and this helps me create a mood from which to decide on how best to pursue my amateurish translation of Walser's story. No matter what, though, no matter how pleased I might be on any given day with my translation of his short work, I can never seem to settle completely on what exactly the writer / the narrator / Walser hoped to achieve by using the word 'skull' in the last third of that work. Today, the word 'skull' has come to suggest to me a type of brittleness. While I read, I find myself running my finger around the upper rim of the socket of my left eye and I imagine this brittleness being shattered. It becomes clear to me today that the bullet from the gunman's rifle in the centre of the image detail on the cover of the Eterna Edition version of Schubert's *Trout Quintet* is not aimed at the deer fleeing up into the woods, but instead is being fired directly between the eyes of Walser as he looks on through the stand of trees that the herd of deer are fleeing towards, and I am witnessing the moment in Walser's story when the fields, meadows, paths, forests, villages, towns and rivers listed in the narrative suddenly become lodged in Walser's skull.

I PIN THE POSTCARD back onto the wall and put the book down. I return to my corridor of record players and amps and speakers, and turn all of the instruments on. Then I lift the needle of the left-hand record player (quintet) at the same time as the needle of the right-hand record player (experimental symphony adapted from quintet). Both machines click on and the turntables begin to spin. I place the needles down simultaneously and listen to the curved spirals of crackle from either side of me. I lift the needles back off.

MY CAREER AS AN ENGINEER splits into two parts – the work I carried out before my sabbatical in Leipzig and the work carried out after. While Catherine was in London that time to present her research at the V&A, she told me she'd bumped into an old colleague of mine, a man called Harry, who'd attended the talk in part to see Catherine, but had also hoped I might be there too. Since I'd heard from him last, he'd joined another firm, one with once long-standing military connections in India that over the years had morphed and expanded into more civilian business arrangements. The firm had received a number of new contracts to design a variety of bridges in northern India, and Harry, this old colleague of mine, he a Mancunian of similar age to me, was putting together a team. He called me one day, telling me that he wanted me involved. I told him I would join on the condition that I could work from Leipzig. I told him I could not work in London again and I did not want to be away from Catherine. Harry agreed, and with that the second half of my career came to life.

I have kept little by way of drawings or notebooks from that time. I dumped all of my notebooks and sketches from the first half of my career when I moved out of my apartment in London. When I then moved from Leipzig to Bilbao, within a year of Catherine passing away, I shed everything except for one drawing and this one notebook I used while designing a concrete road bridge over a gorge in the Meghala province of northern India. I kept the notebook, I think, on account of the job being so modest in cost and scale and perhaps because it was my last. It was also the only bridge I travelled to see during this second part of my career. I visited the site three times – to see the gap we were connecting, to see the bridge scaffolded out in mid-construction and to witness it complete. Within the notebook, two colour photographs are pasted side-by-side, underneath which are some drawings and sketches. The photographs however, are not of the bridge I designed, despite the bridge being, for a concrete bridge, very beautiful. In my mind's eye this bridge appears as an inverted grey convex sliver suspended between two luscious green promontories of forested land. The promontories jut out about forty metres above a dried-up river and are one hundred metres apart. Our bridge cantilevers elegantly out from both sides to a point in the middle of the river valley where the tips of the cantilevers meet. It was a road bridge for local farmers that gave access to the main motorway leading north to the region's capital, and this bridge cut three hours from the travel times these farmers had previously to endure. The photographs in my notebook depict a tiny detail of what were called locally 'living-root bridges'. On my final trip to this region I was brought, as if I were a visiting dignitary, to a village high in one of the mountains behind the southern promontory of our bridge. The local engineers wanted to show me their bridges, formed using the roots of trees. Throughout my correspondences during this job, the local site engineer mentioned these things often to me, so I promised, at the end of the project, when I'd make my final visit to the site that I'd visit these root bridges too.

In the middle of this village were dozens of slim brown bridges at various heights, slung above the roadway below. As we drove into the village in our open-topped jeep, people waved down to us from these bridges and I waved back up. My young site engineer colleague took me to the longest one in the village, it like a huge vine hollowed out and cast across a deep green gorge, connecting the village to the fields and valleys below. It must have been forty metres in length, and as I stepped out onto it I felt no fear. It was a stiff and hard old thing and I would imagine when it rained the longitudinal strands of root would have become quite slippery. She – this young site engineer – then brought me to a smaller root bridge in the process of being constructed and explained how it was done. The roots were chosen from two healthy trees on either side of a valley or river, and the roots were then bent and guided out on an arrangement of bamboo scaffolds to meet each other, whereupon the roots were intertwined and left to grow into each other for months and sometimes years on end until the thing was strong enough to hold a person, or persons, or a motorbike-and-rider, or an ox, or even a small herd. Looking at this bright young Indian engineer turning these intertwining roots in her hands, sweat pouring down my face, I could not help but think what time was like in this place, so, to try and capture something of the time of the place, I took my camera out and photographed twice the section of intertwining root lying across her palm.

The only other particle of my work I kept from this time was a drawing of the concrete bridge I designed across the river valley. It was one of the first layouts I made for the project and it more or less indicated the form, size and scheme of the thing. It was draughted on tracing paper with pencil and ink and it shows the plan, the elevation and three cross-sections of the bridge.

I slip it out of a drawer in my table now and am opening it out across my desktop. The paper is some-what stiff. It doesn't so much flap as creak. It is a pleas-ant sound, like four distant doors of increasing size swinging on their hinges. The folds of the paper apex-ing and valleying across the interface then fall into a tense flatness. If the tracing paper is old enough and has been folded up for long enough, the white fold-lines in the paper remain. This piece of paper is gridded out in an array of perpendicular fold-lines. Tracing paper of course should never be folded. Another engineer, or even an architect, would be abhorred at me for folding a drawing made on tracing paper. Tracing paper should only be rolled, draped or hung. But I knew what I was doing when I folded up and packed away this drawing in my old apartment in Leipzig. I wanted to somehow harm the beauty of the thought that the paper held. At the time I wanted to harm the nature of the thought, I wanted to fold it away into darkness. As I packed up my belongings in my old apartment in Leipzig, in preparation for my move to Bilbao, I wanted to fold away the habit of thinking that had prevailed in my life up to the point of Catherine's sickness and death. I thought that if I could put away the type of thinking I had employed before Catherine's death I might then make room in my person for a type of thinking to help usher me beyond – and perhaps help me forget – the moment of her dying.

When I woke up on the first morning after returning from Catherine's burial in London I was lying on my back, on the floor, beside our bed. The place was quiet and the heating I'd put on the evening before was too high. The apartment seemed over the course of the night to have grown an inch in each direction. The whites of the walls had taken on a pink hue. While I looked at the corners of the bedroom ceiling I became convinced that the room had increased in each corner by exactly one inch along each of the x, y and z axes. I rose, went to our sitting room and slid the vinyl that bore the recording of Schubert's *Trout Quintet* as played by the five East-German musicians out of its sleeve.

The drawing of the bridge in Meghala in northern India was reproduced many times on an old ammonia plotter in a printer's a few streets away from us in Leipzig. I was adept at reproduction of this kind, so the owner of the printer's was always happy for me to do my own copying. Every couple of weeks when I needed to carry out some printing I'd call down and the printer would hand me a mask for the ammonia fumes, lead me to the rear of his premises and leave me there plotting for sometimes hours on end. The plotter was such that as I fed my tracing paper drawing into a long slit at the top, it would be received onto a set of mechanized rollers, which guided the drawing past a wide bright lamp within the machine; concurrently a roll of yellowed paper with a film of ammonia deposited upon it would pass the lamp, thus bleaching everything away, except the slim black lines and lettering from the tracing-paper drawing that obstructed the light of the lamp. Then, as my tracing-paper original re-appeared out of the front of the plotter, a warm blueprint of equal size would curl out of the rear. The upper edge of my original tracing-paper drawing is frayed as a result of this printing, and in places damaged, and the leading corners have the hallmarks of things that were once bent and bent back and flattened and coerced.

The desk I am sitting at now is the one I used in my office in my apartment in Leipzig. It is the only piece of furniture I took from Leipzig to Bilbao. It was left to me by my father, and I only claimed it from my father's office in Ireland once I had begun setting up my workspace in Leipzig. It had been his desk in his back office for dozens of years while he ran his salt- and turf-merchant business. It is a handsome old thing, made from cherrywood, with a stack of three drawers either side and a tabletop with slim ornate panels that edge its underside. It is far smaller than any sort of desk one might purchase or see in an office nowadays. I used it for writing my letters and specifications, and it is where I took any phone calls too. It was placed between the two tall windows to the front wall of the room that became my office, but the desk faced inwards. Beyond the two windows either side, the upper floors of the granite-clad Gutenberg Polytechnic rose into view, and when my back was turned to the thoroughfare and I was working at my desk, I could hear the number 12 tram trundle up and down Prager Strasse. I had a technical drawing board also, and it was angled to the front left of my writing desk. It consisted of a plane of lacquered plywood inclined to a cylindrical steel base. I'd procured it from a closing-down ambulance manufacturer on the southern edge of the city. To the top of the board I'd clamped a cranked lamp, which I could redirect over my head, focusing its oblong of light upon the part of the drawing I was working up or refining.

Along the wall to the left of the drawing board was a dark waist-high bench, a tracing table I'd made with pieces of mahogany I'd found jutting out from a skip one day when I was walking back down from Augustplatz. The table had a large sheet of glass as its top, and below the glass hung two upward-facing shaving lamps. On this table, with the lights beneath shining, I could easily trace drawings or details from other drawings – standard details that I might re-use in other bridges in other parts of India. Along the right-hand wall opposite were two tall bottle-green filing cabinets and two broad metal drawing cabinets for hanging my A1-, A2- and A3-sized tracing-paper originals. At times, during the working day, when the sun slanted through the first-floor windows of my office and I was returning to the room with a steaming cup of coffee or a tea, I would look with admiration on my place of work. This room offered me years of well-ordered thoughts.

My draughting, though, was at first quite poor and I was somewhat ashamed of the first collection of drawing details I posted back to the office in London. They were for a cable-stay bridge in Akker. After six months my draughtsmanship returned to the quality it had been in before my sabbatical, and, from then, my draughting improved towards a type of clarity I find moving because it leads any person who might look at the finished drawing more directly to the thoughts of the person who drew it, through a style of penmanship that comes from a need to be neutral. Some draughters, after inking in their work, often rub out the pencil lines that led to the final form, but I always left these light construction lines, these thinking lines, behind on the paper. It seemed wrongheaded to remove them, and sometimes then on the blueprint I'd later produce from this drawing small traces of the pencil-line substructure would appear here and there.

To the lower edge of the drawing board I'd fitted a timber gutter, and it was into this I placed the variety of clutch pencils, pens (Rotring at first, then Staedler), erasers and blades. To the far end of the gutter I'd store three red felt-tipped markers, and whenever a paper blueprint of a design of a layout or detail of a bridge that I may or may not have been working directly on arrived over from London, I would relish taking the tracing-paper drawing I was engaged with from my board. I would drape it carefully across the glass surface of my neighbouring table. Then I'd unfold this newly arrived paper blueprint out of its envelope and tape it to my drawing board. I would slide these red markers down the gutter towards me and set about checking this other engineer's design and drawing. If I found an error I'd circle it in red.

I was careful to ensure each correction I suggested was followed by an exclamation mark so the person reading this marked-up drawing back in London a few days hence would not be ashamed or hurt or feel in any way isolated or lessened by my concerns. Engineers should create an atmosphere of criticism in their design work – without malice from competitiveness or fear creeping in – and I always considered a circle and an exclamation mark as the cave-painting equivalent of this atmosphere. If I found a drawing to be a particularly strong explanation of what should be built, I would sit to my desk and type a letter to the engineer who produced the drawing, congratulating them on their efforts. If the drawing I received for checking was flawed I would turn the drawing over, tape its corners down and fill the back of the drawing with my handwritten notes explaining my more general thoughts and speculations as to why the approach manifested on the other side did not work. I would imagine any junior engineers, when handed their padded envelope and seeing that it had just arrived back in from Leipzig, must have winced at the first few inches of the drawing appearing from the sheath, them waiting to see if it was filled with or clear of my red marks.

THESE GENTLE BUT CRITICAL discussions are as important to me as any of the buildings or bridges I managed
to successfully leave on the land. I think this is why I
have no difficulty in shedding myself of objects.

It was while I was working in this detached but joy-
ous way that I first came upon the work of the young
Danish engineer. My colleague Harry had informed
me of his talent. This young Dane had come to the fore
in the office because of his ability to solve problems as
they emerged in the 'real time' of building sites. Even
though he was only a year or two out of university he
had become the person most sought-after in the office
whenever something unforeseen had happened on site.
He could see the buildings differently, almost as if they
were sculptures. He could re-imagine and re-direct the
structural forces of a building around mistakes in its
fabric, and he could do this with the smallest and most
graceful of interventions. The principals of two pow-
erful construction companies in the city had already
tried to poach him, but this young Danish engineer
rejected their advances (and their promises of great
remuneration), telling them he wanted to learn more
about the design of bridges, so, our company – keen
to keep him – gave him projects and responsibilities
far greater than someone of his age would usually be
trusted with. In short, and on a number of different
registers, he was adept.

The first set of plans I received from him were almost perfect. It was not just the penmanship or the organization of the viewpoints on the page, but also the content of the design. I remember that day standing at my drawing board and inspecting his schematics for many minutes, my red marker hovering over each cross-section, elevation, detail and specification ... but nothing. I assumed it was another more-senior engineer trying to pull the wool over my eyes until I looked at the initials in the box labelled 'signed off by' – and it said: 'O.V.E.'; initials I had not seen before and could not connect with any engineers I knew. The more the drawings-for-checking kept coming, the more convinced I became of his ability. His solutions were simple. He understood what material was most appropriate to whatever scheme it was he was undertaking. This kind of *feel* for structures usually comes from the experience of visiting completed buildings whose designs you are responsible for; it usually comes from designing a building, then before the framework is closed up one must walk through this skeletal structure and ask oneself in total seriousness: Did I use the correct material in the correct way in each instance here? Though I was an able mathematician and good computational engineer, it took me some years to gain this sense of feel, or to put it another way, it took me some time to add the skills of design to my computational abilities. The skills in design that I eventually gained came from these sometimes lonely and despondent walks through empty building frames I, up till then, had felt I had designed well. I was curious to learn how this young Dane had developed, so young, such sophisticated skills in design. But I never did; I got to know this man only through our correspondence over those years while I had my office in the apartment in Leipzig – me writing letters to him and he responding to me in concise English, with a straight focussed style and at times with flickers of good humour.

I refer to him as young, but he must surely be over forty by now. This, I think, might be the part of what is traumatic in time; holding something in your mind's eye through a type of time – weights falling and rising through a clock tower – that has nothing to do with the instantaneity of the mind's eye. Then two decades or so pass, and the sadness that suddenly takes form is: that time has not only passed for you, but also for the person you remember, but for them time has forked, and one prong of this fork is hard to picture, and this creates an absolute distance. The problem is that I never met, nor even saw a photograph of this young Danish engineer, so all I have is some vague visual sense of a young blond man wearing, let's say, a pair of horn-rimmed glasses.

I heard once, in what was the first phase of my career, a famous architect, whose mediocre designs were proving extremely difficult to build, utter during a meeting with the contracts manager of a site we were working on in Montpellier: 'Building is your problem – I have nothing to do with the workers.' At the time the comment went unnoticed, and the contractor, an obliging man in his late-fifties from Lyon, merely nodded – but I heard it, and it angered me. I wanted to leave the meeting there and then, but as my opportunity to rebut this comment ebbed, I just leaned back from the huddle until my pique subsided. This is what then became important to me in the second part of my career: that the bridges we were designing had no architects involved. I see it sometimes in newspapers, large photographs of bridges that look like other things; a bridge like a harp on its side, a bridge like an upward-facing cross-bow, a contemporary bridge quoting the design of a bridge from a previous era – that sort of nonsense. A bridge is not a trivial structure and shouldn't be put into the hands of an architect. A bridge is an utterance that connects landscapes from which that utterance arrived, and architects know little of the language or materials or the bodies that produce these kinds of utterances.

THE WHINE OF A DRILL SURGES, then blasts like falling brick into my living room. The sound is so sudden and so savage that it feels as if the drill making it is too large for the building to support, and I feel as if the building itself might now crumble around me. The sound beats down in waves from above; then, as quickly as it appeared, it is gone. I wait and listen to a distant clicking until that disappears too. I pause for almost a minute, looking around. I run a finger along another of the creases of the tracing-paper drawing and as I lift my finger off I notice a tremor in my hand. I clench my fist, then run my finger back over the crease again to forget the tremor.

There was a habit I developed over the course of my career of asking myself two very simple questions just before signing off on a final design. The first question was: How might this thing I've designed be built? And the second question was: Am I putting those who will build this design into unnecessary discomfort or danger? This habit was the only thing of value I gave this young Dane, and the job where I relayed the importance of it was near the end of a project he and I had corresponded on for almost ten months. He sent me his final set of drawings for a metal footbridge over a slim distributary of the Ganges running through the grounds of a Christian monastery a hundred miles north of

Calcutta. The bridge was of admirable design. The ratio of bridge-depth to span to load was good and the way the bridge connected to the banks either side seemed to me inventive while also sensitive to the type of rock the banks comprised – a dark brittle granite. The young Dane had integrated the hand-rails of the bridge into the structure so that they, and their criss-crossing metal balusters, contributed to the stiffness of the whole thing, and this then kept the depth of the arcing walkway shallow and grace-ful. The day I received this design I remember push-ing out the corners of the drawing, taping them to my board, turning my lamp on and doing what I always did when I received drawings-for-construction – I imagined the bridge in place, on a breezy day, and me walking over it, then travelling under it, on a boat, say. I imagined the thing being built. The first part of the process was always an enjoyable thing to do. I'd spend sometimes hours in my quiet office sitting on my tall tubular drawing stool considering a design as a thing lifted off the paper. For the young Dane's footbridge I guided my eye in navigations around it first. After this, to help me imagine it being built, I took a sheet of tracing paper and placed it over the Dane's blueprint, and bit by bit traced the elevation and plan of the bridge out in pencil. I lifted the trac-ing paper off the blueprint at regular increments to ensure the fragment I had just traced was buildable, then I added another fragment and imagined how the workers in India would achieve it, then another and another until the bridge completed its span. In this young Dane's footbridge, however, near the end of my checking process, I noticed a flaw, so I picked up my red marker and drew a circle around the point in the structure where two small U-shaped plates were to be, in theory, bolted together and I wrote into the unreachable cavity the young Dane had accidentally designed: 'How will the worker get their hands in there to tighten this bolt?!'

THERE ARE SHOUTS AND HOOTS now coming from above me and another wave of burning roof-bitumen has descended out of somewhere in the blue Bilbao sky. I look out the window to my left. A bird flies by. Then I look back once more at the creases of the tracing paper.

For the first number of weeks here, I stayed in a small guesthouse on Kalea Loteria. It was a family-run place, clean, with narrow rooms overlooking a handsome square and the Santiago cathedral. The bedrooms in the place had no en-suite bathrooms, so each guest had to share the toilet and the shower facilities. I didn't mind, the intimacy reminded me of when I was young. The person next door, though, had a terrible cough and each night for an hour he would hack loudly, over and over, and splutter and blow comedic trumpet-like parps through his nose, then gasp. There were some nights, though, when he coughed so coarsely that I was sure that he might die. This part of town is called the Alde Zaharra, the Old Town, and on the first night, when I went out for a snack, I asked a lady in the small café I'd eaten in to show me where we were located on my tourist map, which sits now in a fold at the back of my notebook. She took the map from me and pored over it for almost five minutes. I was unable to say anything to her and I did not want to take the map from her, because she seemed deep in thought, or at least she was analyzing this simple tourist map as if it were showing her the streets and squares of a place she had never seen before. I wondered if it was possible that she had never looked at a map of Bilbao. Then her husband, the man with whom she seemed to run this café, re-emerged from the back kitchen and she called him over and asked him where on this map we were located. I almost began to laugh – I was sure they were having me on. Then, many minutes later, they exclaimed in near unison and began pointing at the top right-hand corner of the map to a collection of streets all coloured in pink (to demark the '*comercial, monumental, y gastronómico*' part of town), and in among these streets I could make out Kalea Loteria and the Kalea Tenderia, where this café was located, and I realized then that the word *Kalea* was the Basque version of the words *la Calle*, 'the street'.

On the map, to the right of this old and at times touristy part of town, I noticed in the immediate north-eastern district an agglomeration of hospitals, cemeteries and a large church called the Basílica de Begoña. I climbed the hill to this district the next morning and registered with a hospital, knowing that I would require at some stage in the near future the help of a doctor or a nurse of some kind. Then, after a wretched coffee in the hospital canteen, I continued carefully upward to the sandstone basilica. Afternoon Mass was concluding and the congregation of mostly people my age was dispersing outside as I entered the church. I wandered down the dimness of the left-hand flank, crossed the nave, then I sat in the shadows of the opposite flank and took in the gothic patterns across the vaulted ceilings of the place. To my left, in the otherwise empty church, I saw what I first took to be an adolescent boy. He was deep in prayer. Then he began to weep. I looked away, but the boy continued to weep, not uncontrollably, but certainly somewhere near the edge of despair. I wondered what could be troubling so young a man. He wore a navy baseball hat, a pair of shorts, running shoes and a white long-sleeve shirt. Then he rose, hobbled somewhat, gathered up his right arm with his left, and when he turned to me I realized it was a woman in her early forties. Though her eyes were averted, I could tell from the glisten on her cheeks that she was still crying. She faltered past, towards the entrance of the place. Her running shoes, meeting the polished floor tiles of the chapel, issued gentle irregular squeaks as she left. After some time I stood to go. It was still remarkably warm and bright outside. I walked around the side of the church and the grounds opened up to reveal almost the entirety of the city rumbling down to its river valley. I came to a considerable boundary wall to the rear. I peered over, and way below shimmered an oval-shaped swimming pool, surrounded with toy-green AstroTurf, and dotted around this hotel arena lounged near-naked bathers. To their left ran a busy dual carriageway called the Kalea Zabalbide. From my elevated position, the wall that separated the bathers from the thudding streams of road traffic was flattened into a mere line, and for a few seconds I thought: This is how people relax here – they watch rush-hour traffic zooming by. Then, gathering my breath, I looked to the south west of the city and spied a circular green edifice, which I later came to know as the Plaza de Toros, a place I visited one hot afternoon months later to see what happened during a bullfight – a place I haven't visited since. I looked down at the bathers once more. None had moved, and I thought: If I were to come back here in twenty years' time, they might still not have moved, and the traffic that passed might have congealed into a continuous line of carbon.

O

IN MY NOTEBOOK, to the left of the two photographs showing the section of root bridge resting across the young Indian site engineer's hand, there's a pencil sketch I once made absent-mindedly during that time I was in India and away from Catherine. It is of two tiny table-tennis bats – the one on the left is red, the other is black, and a little ball is indicated between them with shiver lines around it.

Catherine was a small, slim person. She had lovely, dark misaligned eyes (the right one straight, the left pointing slightly outward) and she had fine dark hair that she wore up in Grecian plaits around the crown of her head, despite her hair having a parting to the left. She always pulled the cuffs of her jumpers or shirts over her wrists and the heels of her hands, as if she were perpetually on the edge of being cold, and her fingers, each one with a ring, would grasp at the cuffs, which over time would shred beyond repair. When she spoke of serious things she'd frown in what seemed an insincere way, as if at any moment she was about to bring the pretence of her seriousness to an end and smile, and when she listened she'd run her fingertips over her lips and look away, lean her head to one side, then narrow her eyes and raise her eyebrows and, finding her moment, return to speaking. As she grew older she wore fewer rings on her fingers and I noticed her hands grasping less often at the cuffs of her jumpers. I miss her while I am awake and while I am sleeping. I miss her when I rouse at night and when I seek her hand, for a moment, with mine. I thought I would adjust to this absence she carved out of my life, but instead I seem to have curled up into it, and what I look on at now is the ghost of myself wandering about in the hinterlands of that absence hoping that he finds something of her around him, something more tangible than sketches of table-tennis bats in barely used notebooks.

She was a remarkably talented table-tennis player. I was probably average, but because I only played throughout my adult life against Catherine, and because she was far above average, perhaps I wasn't so poor. On the continent it is usual to find one if not many table-tennis tables in almost every public park. These tables are most usually constructed with concrete – the tabletop often has a fin-shaped diaphragm to the underside and a smoothened and sometimes polished upper surface. The lines on the table are recessed and filled with a tough whitened cement. The net is usually a three-inch band of perforated stainless steel. The legs of the tables sometimes consist of two concrete Vs on their sides, or sometimes the supports consist of two upright concrete panels, bolted to the ground, with a large O in the middle of them. I would imagine these table designs vary as much as the local councils that fashion them. It must be an enjoyable job for a local council engineer, designing the table-tennis tables they cast in numbers at a time and organize to be installed in various tree-fringed corners of various municipal and public parks.

There was a park called Brüderplatz about a ten-minute walk from our apartment in Leipzig, and during the middle eight months of the year we would take to it and play. Catherine and I would wander from our apartment, past the bleak concrete-framed ruin on Plato Strasse, into the rumbling and fragrant allotments that adjoined it and out onto the tidy junction between Sternwarte Weg and Brüder Weg, until we arrived, past the stands of *Plattenbau* apartments, at the tree-lined Brüder

Strasse where we'd turn right onto Brüderplatz and venture inward past the beeches and chestnuts that overhung the four table-tennis tables in its centre. Catherine would give me a fifteen-point advantage at the start of each game and if I managed to win I would then start the next game with a fourteen-point advantage. I once reduced that margin to ten, but the game that followed she trounced me twenty-one to eleven. She called it 'the great one-pointer' from there on in. Whenever she'd beat me, she'd call across the table, 'Chin up, chuck!' She'd represented Northumberland at the UK schools' finals when she was seventeen and she was then also presented with the opportunity to train with the UK Olympic team the year after, but she turned it down on account of having received a scholarship to further her studies in Central St Martins.

I REMEMBER CLEARLY one particular moment in one particular game we played in Brüderplatz, and not because it was an especially important point in the game but because the moment always breaks off in my mind's eye into two further moments from my youth, when I used to play table tennis regularly with my sister Edel in the back-yard barn – a shed my father shared with a prosperous local vet called O'Hara.

The moment that triggers these two memories stems from the table-tennis tables in Brüderplatz just after Catherine had, one day, struck a forehand smash towards me. This must have happened on a mid-summer's afternoon because I remember from this moment the sun flaring through the leaves of a tree overhead, the rhombus plane of white-grey concrete of the table-tennis table towards the bottom left, a splash of sky blue emerging from somewhere to the right of my eye and a dab of grey from the underside of Catherine's right foot as she leaned forward to deliver the forehand stroke. But all of this is to the periphery of the image because what commands its centre is the white curvature of the table-tennis ball hurtling towards my eye, it most likely the last thing I registered before I flinched. This image, as I said, never settles – it breaks into two further images, one of which consists of my sister Edel across from me in her dark convent-school uniform playing table tennis one peaceful but cold Friday evening under the fluorescent light of the shed to the rear of my father's house, she shaping to return a backhand back-spin slice to the right quadrant on my side of the table; and the other image contains most prominently the wet white curve of an exposed knee bone of a sheep in dire discomfort that arrived some moments after the image of Edel first formed.

The sheep had been found in a local farmer's barn that night, having given birth alone earlier in the evening to a healthy lamb, and in doing so it had prolapsed its intestines out of its anus. The farmer, a wealthy local man, screeched up to our barn howling for O'Hara. Within a minute our table-tennis table was shoved to one side, a large circle of hay was thrown to the ground and the sheep was lying in the middle of it all, moaning as O'Hara pushed the blood, then the intestines holding the blood, back up into its body. When O'Hara disappeared indoors to get some local anaesthetic for the sheep, he asked me to help the farmer hold the animal in place. 'Hold that ewe's head down or it'll buckle itself,' he whispered, before chasing back out into the yard. As I pushed the sheep's head to the floor I saw its knee bone exposed, this perfectly white curve, like a recently polished billiard jack peering out at me from between the folds of the sheep's skin and its bloodied and dirtied wool. For some reason I can barely remember the smell or the no doubt hideous blueness of the sheep's innards on the floor in comparison to the sharpness with which I can remember, almost seventy years later, that poor ewe's exposed kneecap. The vet returned, and with his muscular, claw-like but graceful hands he injected a few vials of clear liquid into various points on the creature and finished his work. The dazed young ewe was then helped back up into the wealthy farmer's trailer; then, upon thanking and paying O'Hara, the farmer rattled off into the darkness. After this, as if nothing had happened, Edel kicked and brushed the blood-ied hay to one side, rolled our table back out, picked up her bat and ball and said, 'Twelve–twelve, right?'

That night, and for nights later, I dreamt of the whiteness of the ewe's knee, but not with any dread; it would just appear there before me, in the other-wise plumbless blackness of my dreams, this white curve bobbing around, fluctuating in size and quality of gloss. Then, some years later, while I finished my final university exams, it appeared again and I don't remember seeing it since in my sleeping life; I only recall it in my waking life whenever I think of the table-tennis bats I purchased in Leipzig for Catherine, and that particular forehand smash on that particular summer's day in Brüderplatz many years ago.

/\

IN THE LAST WHILE it has occurred to me from time to time that some of the people who visited Brüderplatz over those years when Catherine and I played there must at some juncture have thought: Who is this foreign childless couple playing these intense games of table tennis every weekend in our municipal park?

After these games Catherine and I would sit on a bench, share a bottle of water and watch the players on the adjacent tables. There was a children's playground with a climbing frame in the shrub-lined space opposite and I remember, one afternoon, watching four young boys horsing around in there. Three stood in a line before the fourth, who jogged in zigzags across the width of the playground, darting forward and back, attempting to draw in and elude the other three. On this afternoon the boy managed to evade his playmates. He ran up and over the see-saw in the middle of the park, scrambled through the red climbing frame, sprinted to the stub wall in front of Catherine and me, leapt it, then turned back to his three friends, jumping and calling out, 'West! West, West!' Then this dark-haired boy, panting, rejoined his friends, and Catherine, turning to me, said, 'This place, you know … it's all coming to an end.'

A few mornings before, we'd heard a neighbour being pulled from his apartment. Jürgen was his name. Catherine spoke to him often in the communal stair-well and sometimes invited him to have a cup of tea with us. He'd been a punk in Berlin for years, but after tiring of what he called his *Mauerkrankenheit*, his 'wall-sickness', he moved to Leipzig to work as a typesetter for the *Leipziger Volkszeitung*. He had been warned too often about seemingly inconsequential mistakes and falsehoods about the government appearing in print in this newspaper. A few weeks after he was taken away, Catherine said to me that she reckoned he was also part of the ring that was apparently selling false passports in the disused public toilet at the far end of our street. She said to me once that it must be a struggle to so badly need the thing that you constantly define yourself against.

I used to wonder what my family made of Catherine and I moving to East Germany in the late 1970s and our rare appearances back in Ireland. They never commented on it to me directly. When we visited my sisters – particularly Edel, who remained in B—— all of her life – conversation was almost always a struggle. Restrained distance at close quarters was easy for Catherine, whereas Edel, who could not make sense of it, interpreted Catherine's quietness, this apparent coolness up close, as judgment. One Easter, when we all sat around Edel's kitchen table eating potatoes, peas and ham – in celebration of the tenth anniversary of Edel's marriage to Daniel, a local farmer who I was always fond of – Edel erupted, accusing Catherine, who was not hungry at the time and never ate large meals generally, as having 'notions' for not tucking in to the ham Daniel had prepared (an upturned can of Coca-Cola into a slowly cooked shank). Catherine was completely bemused, whereas a part of me almost agreed with Edel, but I tried to calm things down before someone said something cruel in front of Edel's three gaping children. It was too late, and Edel had already begun to cry and had run from the room. Catherine just looked to me – her mouth having comically dropped open – and I raced down the hallway after Edel. I think maybe having grown up in the industrialized north of England made it easier for Catherine to hold her silence in the close company of others, and this facet of her personality had features that were unrecognizable to Edel, or at least came across to her as 'hard' – they were mysterious to me too when I first met Catherine, but it was her coolness I found attractive. It was something I wanted to approach, to feel what might be warm in it.

She was an only child, and her parents both passed away while we were first going out in London. Her father was cremated, as was her mother. I found the church services that preceded the cremations, in her small Northumberland village, to be peculiar, stern, Protestant affairs. Words like 'precepts', 'criteria', 'laws', 'loci' and 'schema' were spoken out into the quiet of the cold chapel and there seemed to be an utter absence of crying at both events. Catherine rarely spoke about her parents to me, and she seemed glad to get back to London to continue her studies on the history of porcelain production, as if by doing so she could push from her further the possibility of feeling the keenness of these losses. I am sure they came to her some time later, but she never showed me how much they hurt her, or at least I never saw them.

I turn over the page of the notebook and see a tall rectangle full of six-digit numbers. I have no idea what these were once for. Beneath them has been written the word 'feldspar'. I turn the page back, then, with an ache building in my ankle, I slide my chair out, sit, hunch forward and gaze at the polished surface of the wood on the tabletop. There are two dark galaxy-shaped whorls of grain angled away from each other on its surface. Their shapes tell me about the moments when the tree they came from had been cut down. I follow the laminar lines of timber-fibre as they fold and interlace around and away from these small angled galaxies.

In Leipzig we had what might be called a monastically studious life. Catherine would work between her office in our apartment – it sitting to the left of mine – and her office at the Grassi where she got

to grips with what parts of the porcelain collection
the museum owned outright, owned in part and did
not own at all, but had somehow come in posses-
sion of. Most mornings and afternoons she'd spend
in the museum and most evenings she'd spend at
home. We'd dinner at around eight and then either
read in the sitting room together or she'd take her-
self off to her office and listen to her collection of
records, refine her German, which always seemed
perfect to me, or extend her research into the emer-
gence of Meissen porcelain in the early years of the
eighteenth century and the arcanist she told me
about often, this Stöltzel, who sometime in the early
1700s apparently broke ranks with Meissen and fled
for Vienna with his pregnant mistress. According
to Catherine, it was in Vienna that Stöltzel helped
bring into being the other European powerhouse
of porcelain production, Du Paquier, and in effect
stole the methods and recipes from Meissen; and
this, if I am remembering it correctly, then made it
necessary for Meissen to create trademarks for each
of their works – an intertwined A and R, and the
two crossed swords, which still exist today hand-
painted in cobalt blue on the surface of their objects.
This Stöltzel fascinated Catherine, but she felt, with
the volume of work required of her position at the
Grassi, that she never satisfied her curiosity in him,

particularly when it became clear that to fill out the story of Stöltzel would require regular trips to a variety of archives in Vienna. Her sense of duty to the Grassi kept her compulsions at bay and led her instead towards the history of hard-paste porcelain, particularly the china clay used in its production, this 'gaoling' she often mentioned that, apparently, is also important in the production of certain types of paper with grades of permeability better suited for holding printed ink. It was around this time, though, soon after she retired and was about to embark on this research into Stöltzel, that her stomach began to hurt and she began to feel unwell. We enjoyed our work, though, and we enjoyed the depths the narrowness of our disciplines could take us.

When I compare those busy years up to Catherine's illness to the years when I first arrived in Leipzig, it would seem to me that during those five or so years of my sabbatical I had entered a kind of mania. I still have not managed to totally clarify this in myself, but for a person to abandon their career so completely, and when I compare my scattered indistinct memories from this time to the near decade-and-a-half I spent after my sabbatical working with great pleasure as a bridge engineer, then I assume that I, at least for some period of this sabbatical, had lost my bearings. I've tried often, but I remember little from this time and I can only surmise that my guilt at my old colleague's suicide had driven what focus I had from me.

WHEN I ARRIVED FIRST in Leipzig in the late 1970s the place was subdued, and it felt badly emptied out too. The city was so sedate that I think my guilt-ridden disquiet expanded too easily into its silences; and the streetscapes, especially those down at the southern end of Prager Strasse, must have seemed disproportionately brutalized and incoherent to me. There was one day, at the nearby St Paul's neo-Gothic cathedral, which the local community had then taken upon themselves to rebuild, when I walked up onto the western plaza of the cathedral just as a flat-trailer lorry had rolled away to reveal its final delivery of the day that I saw fifty freshly cast, seven-foot-tall gargoyles squatting in ordered rows in front of me. I walked through their gri-maces, grimaces not intended to be viewed so closely, grimaces meant only to be viewed from a distance below. There was a jackhammer somewhere nearby blasting stone to pieces. This horrible din followed me as I continued past the gargoyles, the scaffold shrouding the southern elevation of the church, and as I made my way up to the junction between Bayreuther Strasse and Gericht Strasse. Here, the narrow streets opened out, and the planar blond communist *Plattenbaus*, the neo-Gothic hysterics of the churches and the Bavarian-styled train station in the near distance conflated into phantasms of composite buildings that gathered and mounded into the gaps between those that were actual. Then, dazed, I came upon a final edifice across the broad bleating road junction. It was a stocky cylindrical thing with the words, *Hier steht Tod im dienst des Lebens*, 'Here lies death at the service of life', written across the head of its entranceway, and with this I fell into what felt like a new kind of quiet. I returned home and the void I associate with this period of time must then have begun gathering me in, because all I can remember from each day during these years was two activities. The first half of the day I would wander around the city with a notebook and pencil and sit and draw and redraw in chiaroscuro a small collection of architectural details peculiar to each place. Then, underneath each drawing I'd list the street name and I'd scribble a brief description of how the building surrounding the detail – that did not wholly appear in my drawing – might once have been constructed.

Though I threw away the notebooks I filled doing this pointless task, the details of which I have largely forgotten, I can still claim that I once knew the very centre of Leipzig more intensely than anyone ever has. (These drawing details appear to me now in fragments, like a bedraggled mound of parts from a series of ornate buildings, built only to be toppled one upon the other.) In the afternoons I'd return to the apartment and lunch lightly. Afterwards I'd take out a dozen rolls of paper tape of various colours and draw a truss or some brightly coloured trussed shape across the walls of the room that a few years hence would become my office. I'd work until Catherine came home; then I'd show her my notebook and wall-drawings from the day. And she'd nod and say quietly that she was glad I was keeping busy. Many years later she told me that during this time she, having registered officially with the state, had twice been visited at work by Stasi police officers enquiring about my movements through the city, and she told me that she at first told them I was a freelance lecturer in the history of engineering, but on sabbatical from my post in London to research Leipzig's urban planning and buildings. Then, two years later, when they began again to track my movements, these Stasi officers confronted her once more, and this time she admitted to them that I was once a structural engineer who worked in London and the stress of this career had led me to a state of crisis followed by this prolonged state of some mental agitation – a situation lengthened, I realize, by my searching for patterns in the city where there were none to see. The Stasi followed me for six months afterwards, still photographing me drawing and nosing around. Sometimes they would steal into our apartment while Catherine and I were out. They would photograph and document these colourful trusses I made on the walls, as if these Stasi officers, in their far-greater paranoia, could somehow discern a pattern from my failure at finding one. They eventually deemed me harmless and soon after left me alone. I learned of these intrusions one afternoon in the early 2000s when Catherine and I visited the Stasi HQ in Berlin, a few years after they had made public their files from the whole era. We were on our way to London for a conference to which Catherine had been invited to contribute. We didn't leave ourselves enough time, but we still wanted a glimpse, to see if the Stasi had perhaps made a file on us over those years. And of course they had. One was on Catherine, a profile, a photograph and a record of her trips over and back to London. There were two files on me, one consisted of photographs and notes of my movements during the first five years of my time in Leipzig – a strange folder to sift through, which included photographs of me with my hair unkempt and long, then shorn off, then long again, then shorn off once more; a series of photocopies of drawings attributed to me depicting a leaf bud coming into bloom on a tree I must have fixated on over the course of one spring; a photograph of me hunkered down at the foot of a crane; and a range of photographs of these wall drawings I made in our apartment. The other file held a microfiche of all of my correspondence while I was designing and checking the schemes and details for the up on twenty bridges my company produced for that construction firm in northern India: faxes, phone calls, letters and drawings from 1983 to early '89.

In any case, near the end of this period of sabbatical in Leipzig it began to dawn on me that these enormous colourful trusses I had been drawing and stripping off and drawing again back onto the wall of our apartment were changing in nature. It was as if the chiaroscuro notebook drawings from earlier in the day were beginning to inflect themselves upon the flatter and more diagrammatic drawings on the wall. The diagrammatic drawings were developing, or bending themselves into perspectival drawings of unknown objects that sat somewhere between being a flat truss and a rendering of a rectilinear three-dimensional form of some strange kind – not dissimilar to how a drawing of a hexagon and a cube coalesces and departs depending on how you look at it. Then, once I exhausted this two-and-a-half-dimensioned style of drawing, it seems, from what I remember of what Catherine told to me about this time, that I had become calmer and was sleeping more evenly. It was soon after this that I received the phone call from Harry, my old Mancunian colleague, about coming on board with his bridge-design team. It occurs to me now that Catherine, in her own subtle way, nursed me back into production, and I realize now too that it was probably at this time that the keenness of the loss of her parents had struck her, and it saddens me to think that I was unable to help.

THE TENDONS over my kneecaps are stiffening, so I stand, shake my legs out and lean against the table. I look up from my notebook and gaze at the wall. To my left is the postcard of four Alpine peaks. Further to the left again, light from the tall windows that look onto my small balcony breaks across the imperfections of the paint on the wall. As I remove my glasses, everything in front of me softens. I look back at the wall and it appears no more revelatory than seconds before when I was wearing my glasses. In Walser's '4' the word he speaks to the wall in front of him is *täuschen*, 'to deceive'. At first I thought this word was *tauschen*, 'to swap'. I think if Walser meant just to deceive, then the narrator would pass through the wall and continue on his journey intact, as it were, as he travelled over the 'fields, meadows, paths, forests, villages, towns, rivers', but I think Walser intended something of the word *tauschen* to haunt the word *täuschen*, as if he wanted his reader to understand that the narrator was at once deceiving the wall and swapping with it. I believe that he deceived the wall first, then with these various places from the land outside trapped within his skull, he returned to the wall of the narrator's room, the one where the emptied-out narrator (his second self) sits staring, and onto this he projected the nature of what he saw outside to the emptied-out narrator sitting in his chair waiting to gaze on at it.

I replace my glasses, push my two fingers onto the timber swirls of grain below and consider that perhaps it's best, now the heat has long gone from my waking, that I leave the young Danish engineer as he is – to save him this wild-goose chase around France and India checking my work. It's better my dreams of these buildings from my past continue to trouble me at night and that I wake suddenly to the groans of collapse, because at least then it will keep the regrets and mysteries of my life at bay for longer, out in the hinterlands of my memory, where they are unable to coagulate or gather into coherent images that might visit me in the day or night. Images of this kind (images I am uninterested in and maybe even afraid of seeing) gather in those places beyond where the bogs have been cut, beyond B——, where the baroque skyways of electricity lines have been drawn – these more fearful images develop in the quiet interstices of land beyond and between the roads. It would be wise for me to stay on the road. At least then, when I wake to these bloated anxieties, I know where I am – on the dried-out routes of my own construction.

I lift my fingers from the galaxies.

BEFORE CATHERINE FELL ILL we took two trips. One was to Bamberg in Bavaria and one to Princeton in the United States. Catherine wanted to visit an observatory on the hills of Bamberg and she wanted to see also a set of Richard Serra's curved steel sculptures, *The Hedgehog and the Fox*, which had by then been installed for over a decade on the grounds of the university in Princeton. She told me she wanted to enter the observatory on her own, but that she'd like to walk around Bamberg town with me. We took her then new Praktica camera with us on the trip. She found a small stone plaque on the side of a building on the southern incline of Bamberg, carved in memoriam to a German philosopher I know near nothing about called Hegel. She took a photograph and came back the next day and she took another. These, and the photographs she took within the observatory, were the only ones she made with that camera while we were on our trip. They all sit in a paper wallet on a shelf on the wall behind me. She said she always loved the title of the steel sculpture in Princeton, but that it was 'no use at all admiring it from afar'. She wanted to navigate around it, to touch it. She said she wanted me to walk around it and to touch it with her too.

The work in Princeton struck me as a really fine piece of engineering. Three broadly curved S-shaped strips of rusting Cor Ten steel on their sides, all almost twelve feet tall and kept upright by the fact of their inertia and curvature. There is a gap of a metre or so between each, and such is the gentle irregularity of the curves that this gap sometimes narrows alarmingly and sometimes opens out in a most expansive manner. The sculpture stands near the university football stadium. When we visited that summer, the campus was subdued. For hours, even though Catherine's strength was beginning to fail, we walked up and down these things, sometimes meeting each other but more often not. The next morning we travelled back to New York and went to a show on Broadway whose name and content I have forgotten. A few days later we flew back to Berlin, whereupon we returned to our apartment in Leipzig and over time converted Catherine's office, which neighboured my once office space, into a bedroom for her to rest in; and over the course of the following year, with the regular company and guidance of the nurses and doctors from Leipzig's St Elisabeth Hospital, she left me. Each day, during this time, we hugged each other like bewildered children, and I remember us also in calmer moments watching a VHS recording of a film called *The Great Ecstasy of Woodcarver Steiner*. It is a documentary made by Werner Herzog for West-German television back in the early Seventies about a Swiss ski-jumper – this Steiner – who could jump farther than any other ski-jumper in the world at that time. The film is a lovely thing, showing tall slim competitors taking flight, one after another, soaring through the mountain air and landing sometimes with great grace and sometimes in scared, clumsy and painful twists, as if they are scrambling desperately after their own centres of gravity. As we watched it one afternoon, and while one of the ski-jumpers featured in the film slipped as he left the upward-curving lip of the ski-slope and moments later plunged groundward, knocking himself into an unconscious limpness, Catherine turned to me and said how beautiful she always thought our apartment to be.

A number of months after she had passed on, I was loitering around the apartment not knowing quite what to do. I sat down on Catherine's bed and leafed through an art magazine from a stack she'd left on a table at the front corner of the room. I found some photographs of this Richard Serra's work and around the photographs of these great steel corridors was a Q&A with some leading academic in art history. I alighted on a quote from Serra: 'Being lost throws you back on yourself, and it makes you anxious to have to choose a direction without knowing where you'll end up.'

Despite what is comforting in this, I neither seek nor find solace these days from walking around Serra's steel sculptures in this Guggenheim Museum in my Bilbao. The first time I encountered these sculptures it was a Monday. The museum, unbeknownst to me, was closed. I had wandered around the building trying to find the main entrance, but instead, behind one of the curves of the façade I found a service-entrance door held open with a wedge of timber. I entered and I think the cleaners and service staff working there mistook, and have continued mis- taking, me for a local artist of some importance and who has been given access to the gallery on a Monday. At the entrance to the main gallery inside, the red- brownness of the more complex sculptures became apparent. They seemed almost welcoming, like they were bronzed giants sitting around a table, their arms curved out in front of them awaiting my presence. (These sculptures, though, look nothing like giants' arms, these sculptures look like large curved units of steel arranged in a way Richard Serra aimed for.) I walked into Serra's first arrangement – a torc of many swirls. The way this bending corridor of steel opened up and closed over and leant in on me brought me to the edge of dizziness. Fearful, I turned, without reach- ing the centre of the work, and made my way back to the outside of the brown steel cocoon. For the whole next week or so I stalked, like a scalded cat, around the perimeter of all of these objects. I hardened to them in the way an engineer must harden to their own structures, as if looking at the work of a great enemy, ready to pounce on the smallest of errors. The sculptures then became structures sitting on an exhausted alien landscape awaiting my appraisal and signing-off. First thing each day I looked down at them from the gallery above and then I walked around them again, making mental notes and trying to prepare myself for entering the first arrangement once more.

These days, when I arrive at the gallery I still go and stand on the first-floor balcony and survey the eight maze-like arrangements laid out across the ground below. Some of the arrangements are enclosed coiled walls, some are single arcs, some torcs, some elongated esses, one merely a row of single-radius curves arrayed one after another. I now have a system for the order in which I visit them. I want, for as long as I am able to visit these things, to approach them in a different order each time. I number the arrangements '1' to '8' and I approach each discrete object only from the left-hand side. The problem is that despite these constraints there are still 8! different versions of approach to this entire work: 40,320 different permutations, which by my reckoning is over 110 years at one visit a day, or at two visits a day it is just over fifty-five years. Four visits a day is almost twenty-eight years. But I am usually exhausted after one visit. I will never see out my system.

Another system that might produce a way for gathering these objects in would be to ascribe each arrangement a note on an octave and visit the works in the order of a musical composition that I might draw from my own narrow experience of music, or one simple self-penned composition I might consider suitable to the mood of the place generally. What is important to both of these thorough if artless systems is that I want to push back against Serra's wish that these things might make you feel lost; I have no interest in entering into Serra's fabrications-of-anxiety. I only have interest in systematically grinding the experience of these wonders in engineering down to instances in the past that I barely remember, but can justify to myself as ticks on a sheet of paper beside a stack of numbers.

The order I visit the works these days revolves around the fourth permutation within Order 8! and is, for today: 1, 2, 5, **4**, 3, 6, 7, 8, which leads on from yesterday's permutation: 1, 5, 3, **4**, 2, 6, 7, 8. Whereas the beginning of this Order 4 within Order 8! would have taken the preceding form of: 5, 2, 3, **4**, 1, 6, 7, 8. This Order 4 renders the fourth sculpture as a still point at the centre of my current daily navigations. These shrinking orders will eventually lead to Order 1 of Order 1! I write out each permutation ten in advance. Each day after I finish my walk through the work I write out a new permutation, always keeping them ten in advance, so that anyone who might need to piece together the simple pattern and direction of this system can do so, replicate it, and maybe complete it for me.

1, 5, 3, **4**, 2, 6, 7, 8
1, 2, 5, **4**, 3, 6, 7, 8
1, 2, 3, **4**, 6, 5, 7, 8
1, 2, 3, **4**, 7, 6, 5, 8
1, 2, 3, **4**, 8, 6, 7, 5
6, 2, 3, **4**, 5, 1, 7, 8
1, 6, 3, **4**, 5, 2, 7, 8
1, 2, 6, **4**, 5, 3, 7, 8
1, 2, 3, **4**, 5, 7, 6, 8
1, 2, 3, **4**, 5, 8, 7, 6
7, 2, 3, **4**, 5, 6, 1, 8

The piece I've numbered '8', the last piece of Serra's works, is my favourite. It is the arrangement that most admits to the discontinuousness of its elements. The steel plates in this sculpture meet each other at angles that are near to perpendicular. This is unlike any of the other pieces, which are an arrangement of parts that are either totally separate, like in piece '7' (a number of separate sheets arranged, domino-like, one after the other), or, for the remaining pieces, where the sheets run into each other so as to suggest continuousness. The corners of '8' make it feel almost house-like. Even though the centre of the work leads to a corner, an end of sorts, it is an end that you have to turn from and leave, and this has the effect then of re-igniting the whole place, the whole city, and leading you to quickly forgetting that corner at the end of the sculpture as you walk out along the corridors of dark steel until you are deposited back into the bright and open arena again. I once overheard a tour guide – standing in the middle of the coils of arrangement '2', he circled by a crowd of tourists and enthusiasts – say that Serra's works are 'imageless, they are pure experience'. I wondered for weeks how someone who looked to be an authority on these works could say such a thing. The works are full of images, particularly the tilted torc arrangements. While I move through their sweeping bending corridors, reformulating the rusted steel-world as I go, I imagine a version of myself standing at the entrance to the work, but because I can never be certain as to exactly where the entrance is relative to where I am at any moment within the coils, I place the entrance in my mind at every point to my left as I enter the coils and every point to my right as I leave them.

The five torc-shaped pieces have an entirely different surface finish to the pieces with simpler curves. The torc-shaped pieces, or '1', '2', '3', '5' and '6', have three and sometimes four curvatures in them, whereas the pieces I number '4', '7' and '8' have one, and sometimes two curvatures to them. In making the more complex pieces, the iron content of the steel must have had to be increased, or the amount of coolant poured onto the surfaces of the works as they were being manipulated was far greater. When I run my hand along the surfaces of '1', '2', '3', '5' and '6', the sensation is similar to what one might feel while rubbing the rust off a sheet of metal; it is rough, but no rust ever comes loose. Whereas, when I run my hand along '4', '7' and '8' the surface is smoother, cooler even. So too, the surfaces are far darker, and this makes these objects seem heavier. Perhaps the iron ore extracted to make these objects came from a mine far distant to the other. In any case, the thickness of each plate of each object is the same, all about the distance from the middle knuckle of my index finger to its tip. This thickness is of uninterrupted steel, so if that thickness is 5.5 centimetres and the height of each work is 4 metres, then the mass of a plate 30 metres in length is 0.055 metres by 4 metres by 30 metres by 7,850 kilogrammes per cubic metre (the density of steel), which would make a single plate, of 30 metres in length: 51,810 kilogrammes – almost 52 tonnes. One hundred and four tonnes, then, is the quantity that sometimes runs through my head when I pass through a corridor of this canting steel. I don't consider these objects, though, as things of large weight. I've dealt with larger numbers and larger weights adeptly over the years. I have witnessed teams of workers handle forms and weights of greater complexity and size. But I find Serra's steel sculptures offer me a transition away from the work I carried out in the latter half of my career, the work after my sabbatical, and towards the slowing, flattening then concaving of my activities and thoughts into the form I see as a future obsession – I am moving these days from an obsession with the concave form of the upward arc of the bridge to the convex form of the arc turned over.

I ANGLE THE CHAIR at my desk out into the room, sit on it and stretch my arms out above me for ten seconds, then I reach my arms out before me, then I bend forward and try to reach my outstretched feet. I do this three times down the middle of my body, then I lean my body to the right and do it once, then I lean my body to the left and do it once again.

I gather my breath, go to the wall opposite and lay my palm flat against it at shoulder height, step forward and stretch out my shoulder tendons and the muscle that connects my shoulder to my chest bone. Then I do this to the other shoulder, then over and back, thrice again. This wall separates me from the apartment next door, a place that has lain empty for as long as I have lived here. Sometimes at night I imagine a large dark upright torus, a donut-shaped thing, standing silently in the next room and the hole at its centre gently sucking me towards it, or towards some future catastrophe beyond it. I think this shoulder-stretch at the wall is the best stretch when it comes to posture, it pulls the whole body back into an upright position, it extends the dominant pectorals – the muscles, which, if your life is sedentary, pull your shoulders into the rounded stoop most old people, I notice, suffer from. I still stand somewhat upright and this I believe has had good repercussions for the rest of my body, my hips, my knees and my digestion. Other than some stiffness and pain in the morning when I rise from bed, by the time I leave the house I usually feel like I am limber and neat.

When I am out and about in this part of the city I have spoken-Basque merely sufficient to order food and certain drinks. At first I tried to learn some Spanish, but I grew quickly uninterested because of the pleasure I had already derived from learning German. I found with German that the view of the world was from a fascinating new direction. I would say when learning German I felt like I was placed to the north east of things, whereas when I began to learn Spanish I felt like I was placed to the south west of things, a position that was not exotic enough for me on account of its similarity to the position I give the English language, which I place at the west-south-west of things

– so I gave up. Basque, however, has no ordinate for me; it is total confusion – TK, XK, XT – I mime words and point at things, but I prefer this form of annexation to becoming proficient in Spanish. I'd imagine if my fellow Old Towners here had to trade, they'd prefer me ignorant of Basque if that meant me also ignorant of Spanish. There's a strange and singular grammatical case I've heard of in this language that puzzles me often, though. It's called the ergative case, and from what I've gathered it creates sentence structures where the core of the transitive verb leans away from the subject and towards the object. So a sentence like: 'The woman has seen the man,' then would be in this ergative case: 'Woman the | man the | seen | has,' or a sentence like, 'The man has given the child a book,' would be: 'Man the | child the | book the | given | has.' This oddness happening in near silence on the streets around me raises my spirits, almost out of my body.

ON THIS FOURTH WALL of my sitting room hangs a small rectangular mirror and a narrow, L-shaped shelf made of tulip wood. Some days I place a candle on the shelf, but more often I place a flower or flowers. Today there is a thin glass of water with a white tulip resting in it. The tulip will soon have to be changed.

One of the petals has drooped so low – like a dislocated mandible – that it will probably disengage and topple by evening. The hanging petal reveals the flower's stamen and pollen – the black and yellow guts of the thing. Behind the thin glass of water leans the white paper wallet containing the photographs Catherine took during her time in the observatory on that hill in Bamberg. I do not consider these things as my possessions. And because she asked me not to accompany her into the observatory that time we visited Bamberg I have always assumed that what she photographed might not be for me to look at either. Despite this, I have not thrown them away, or hidden them. They sit up here every day, these images, in some sort of sequence, leaning lightly against each other in the darkness of this paper wallet, behind a candle, or more usually a glass of water, most often holding a tulip.

I consider her bag under my shirts in the drawer in my bedroom and the large envelope inside, full of our slips of paper. I take the wallet from behind the glass holding the tulip, walk over to my armchair – still placed between the two sets of record players, amps and speakers – and open the wallet out on my lap.

The first photograph is over-exposed and contains a series of soft vertical lilac lines to the bottom right-hand corner. The next three photographs are of total blackness, as if Catherine had forgotten to take the cap off the camera lens. I wonder for what reason she left these layers of white then black, black, black in the wallet. It is the sort of thing she would usually have binned. Perhaps at the time she saw something poetic in opening these twenty-four or so exposures with a near-white, then three black, glossy rectangles. The next image is of her feet stilled in the act of walking across a floor covered over in glowing parquet. Her right foot protrudes down from the top right-hand corner into the middle of the image, while her left foot trails in a slight bend behind. She is wearing dark nylon trousers and a pair of closed-toed sandals. It is as if the right foot is about to take her weight and her left foot is about to scissor past her right. The movement of her legs and the stillness of the parquet flooring below suggests that she is accelerating towards some unknown place, as if she has just been called from what I presume to be the waiting room in the observatory, and while fumbling with her camera, which she was in no doubt preparing for the inner chambers of the observatory, she accidentally took this photograph of her feet. The next photograph is blown-out again, another panel of almost total white, but still I look at it. I imagine her taking this photograph and for a sore moment I try to imagine what it is she was trying to record for me to see. I close over the wallet and look to the wall. I look to the wall for some time. I can hear the building creak around me, gentle stirrings as the early morning heat touches the envelope of the thing, the cladding, the windows, the doors: expanding them carefully, like a long intake of breath over the course of the day, before evening time when the building begins to exhale again and returns to the form of its rest.

I open the wallet and flick the white panel down to reveal the next image: a set of steps with timber balusters ascending on either side. I pick the photograph up. The steps in it are covered over in carpet with a Victorian pattern, worn down the middle but seemingly untrodden upon at the edges. The steps lead to a landing, beyond which is an entrance to a room with the door ajar, and for an instant this stairway reminds me of the day my eldest sister Jo chased me up to the water closet of our home in the Midlands and grabbed me before I could hide. I had been meddling with her colouring pencils, which she liked to keep in a specific order on her dresser – all of them pared to the same length all of the time. She grabbed me, furious, turned me towards her, gathered some sputum and spat it into my face. She thumped back down the stairway and I stood for some moments in shock, then I turned and left to clean my face off in the sink in the water closet behind. I flip the card over and see a simple note in Catherine's handwriting – *stairwell to first chamber*. I flip back to the rear sides of the other non-images and all are without notes except for the blown-out white image before the image of the stairwell. Written onto the rear of this photograph are the words: *observatory, Sternwarte, Stern warten, to wait for stars, to sit and wait for stars.*

I flip to the photograph after the photograph of the stairwell but it is so duskily black that I can barely make out what it is trying to depict. I turn it over and there is nothing. I flip to the next and it shows, in the centre of the image, a small mechanical model of the Earth and Moon. Behind the object is a white chart covered in neat columns of eight-digit numbers the meaning of which I can make no sense of from the picture. The photo is not so well composed. The vertical piece of steel holding the tiny Moon, as if at arm's-length away from the bronzed and near-featureless surface of the Earth, is leaning to the right. Looking at that slim tube of out-of-plumb metal makes me for a moment feel unwell, almost dizzy. I turn the picture over and it says merely: *Earth and Moon*. The next image is completely black and so is the next. I then alight on a handsome image of a timber tabletop, around which are scattered a miscellany of papers. In the middle of the table is another mechanical model. This time it is of Jupiter and its fifty-three moons, all arranged with various spoke-like prongs around this flawless ball of what seems to me to be ivory, itself inclined into a broad circular band of brass set onto three turned-timber legs of what I would guess is mahogany or teak. The bases of the timber legs have been carved into sculptural figures of female deities of a kind that represent things like fertility, resurrection and imperial power. There is a sash window behind the table. Beyond it sunlight breaks through the trees and in the distance it is possible to make out the red slanting roofs of Bamberg below. I picture myself pacing around on the street outside waiting for Catherine to re-emerge.

To the rear of the photograph a note says that the ball is made from porcelain and that the moons are ivory spheres. In brackets after this note she has the words *COLONIALISM OF THE COSMOS*.

The next three photographs are variations of the previous one and the next shows a close-up of the mechanism that spins the arms carrying the moons that orbit Jupiter. This machined part I imagine spins slowly each time Jupiter itself is rotated. The next photograph shows one of the tiny rotating gears to the underside of one such moon. This gear rotates this moon as it traces its synchronous orbit of Jupiter. I admire the deductive style of Catherine's looking. Then I flick to the next photograph and I can see it is of me halfway across a street in Bamberg. I am looking away from the camera, surveying the road as I cross. It is not a particularly special photograph, but I can tell from it immediately that I have since lost weight and some more of my hair. To the rear there is an extended note in cramped lettering.

I stood between two cars for this one. I was waiting for you to reappear from the pharmacy. I thought it would be nice in this light to see you cross over towards me. I stood for a long while looking through the camera and waiting. I learned that this focussing time of photography is very strange indeed. Then, down the eyepiece I saw a man who looked like you, but who was much younger. I peeked over the camera for a moment to check if it was you, but then I lost my place and of course you then appeared from the entrance to the pharmacy, but I was still following the younger man, and when I went back to taking the photograph you were already halfway across the road and looking in the other direction checking to see if any cars were coming. I was sure this photograph would be blurred, but I am really glad it is quite sharp, even though your face is not visible.

I turn the photograph back over and see the slant of evening light falling across the street and upon the cars and façades beyond, and I reckon, had Catherine not been interrupted by that younger man built similarly to me, she would have taken a handsome picture of me and I would be looking at this handsome version of myself crossing that road instead.

The next two photographs are of the plaque carved out to this Hegel. It sits at mid-height on the first-floor corner of a building of cut stone. The first photo is brighter than the second and the plaque sits fractions to the left of centre, and if I were to frame or show one of these photographs to anyone I would show the second – the colours are somewhat less blown-out, more sumptuous even.

The following photograph is blacked-out and so are these last three. There is one more and then one more after that. The next photograph is of a rather bleak industrial five-storey building in a state of ruin. I don't recognize it, and it is not from that trip. It is neither a Bavarian nor an American building. There are railway lines to the foreground and just beyond are stacks of timber sleepers strewn over each other in repeated mounds, almost like dunes, that run up to the front entrance of this dilapidated old factory with kicked-in doors and broken windows. The façade shows glimpses of beige-yellow between the vast island-like patches of dust that cover the building, which is otherwise completely symmetrical. Along the upward-curving pediment in the middle of the elevation are three indistinct words, then one I can make out as FABRIK. I have no idea what this factory might once have manufactured, the shape of the building tells me little of what might have happened inside. The last photo then is of flat industrialized land, with a range of single-storey and partly collapsed lean-to buildings made of concrete and rusting iron, and beyond that are plains of blackened soil and further railway tracks with power lines stretched out overhead. On the rear of this photograph are the words, written in blue biro, *Naumburg to Leipzig*, and below those: *Beneath it lies dread all the same, and also beneath it lies despair, and when the spell of illusion is broken, when life begins to quake, then it is immediately apparent that despair was what was lying beneath. – Kierkegaard*.

Then to the right-hand side, written in Catherine's forward-slanting handwriting, are three German words.

Two	Zwei
Doubt	Zweifel
Despair	Verzweifeln

I am almost disappointed in her. I am disappointed that she had accepted what seems to me to be a spatialization of despair that suggests meaning comes from depth. It seems in her loneliness she accepted despair as being underneath something else, deeper even. Despair is a surface entity that pools into and around all other feelings of intensity. It is the intensity with which it ruptures that gives it its apparent force. For some reason Catherine seemed, in her last few months, to have begun ascribing intensity and meaning to depth, or deep feelings, as if all of a sudden she was inhabiting a house, one ordered in the hierarchies of the upper classes. I don't ever remember her reading or mentioning to me this Kierkegaard, of whom I have heard, but of whom I have almost no knowledge other than that he seems to be a kind of go-to man for illustrating great depths of feeling. It seems to me he didn't have the depth of decency to realize the intensity of his shallowness, it seems to me he wanted to keep himself impressed by the apparent great depths of his feelings; that he wanted to devote himself to his own self-envy. Or perhaps I am just jealous that she turned to him. I fold the wallet over and begin to rise, then I open the wallet back out again and I lift the photograph depicting the top of the Victorian stairway in the observatory out and consider putting it up onto a wall in the room, so that when I pass it later today or some day in the near future I can look on it, if only to remind me of the feeling of my older sister's warm spray of sputum on my face. I return it to the wallet, Jo was a good sister to me, and instead I pick out the totally over-exposed image before it. I take the image out and close over the wallet. I put the wallet back onto the shelf, leaning it against the wall behind the thin glass of water holding the fraying tulip and bring the over-exposed image to my desk, lift a drawing pin from a drawer and pin the photograph up alongside the postcard holding the image of those Alpine peaks with their names and heights above sea level gathered up in the heavens. It is a handsome diptych. One a taut outward curve of glossy white, the other a faded range of greys, whites and blacks. I shift my weight over and back and watch the light from the window to my left spill across these surfaces pinned to the wall. The panel to the left, the postcard, is older and there are more creases on it. When I move like this, over and back, it throws up more play. The green reflecting from the trees and buildings outside and the tiny hint of sky blue from between the trees is pooling in one of the facets created by an imperfection on the surface of the postcard.

The last time I saw my brother Allen was on a bench along the Royal Canal in Dublin. It was a sunny afternoon and we were both on a rare visit home. By then, he was almost two years door-stepping and photographing criminals for a tabloid newspaper he worked for in London. He looked haggard and spent. His blue eyes were tired, his beard greying and hair receding, but he spoke to me about his projects with excitement, as if what he had lost in trying to make art he had replaced with danger and disruption and in causing upset to the criminals, who were deemed deserving of this upset, through the tabloid whose employ he was under – their bloated faces splayed all over the front pages of newspapers each morning. I think eventually the righteousness of his employers must have percolated into him. We were sitting close to each other beside the part of the Royal Canal that runs just south of Drumcondra station, where he was soon to go to board the Sligo train back to the Midlands to visit our sister Edel, her three teenage children and her pleasant and large-handed husband, Daniel. Allen and I talked about our father and the way he dissolved over the years after our mother passed away. Allen said he still felt guilt for how he was too young and too sad to offer any sort of support to him – he being the only one of us siblings left in the house by the end. I listened in silence. The water in the canal was at times oily then at times these puddles of oil would come apart and float off towards the lock gushing in hidden echoes a hundred yards or so to our right. I think Allen knew, from perhaps talking to Catherine, that I had been in a delicate state for the preceding years and out of care for me he asked nothing but the most superficial of questions. When I told him I was back working again, but this time from my office in my apartment in Leipzig, he peered at me with a grave look on his face, which then fell into an almost rueful smile. I realize that he realized when I told him of this development that I had come out of whatever it was I had fallen into. I can only imagine how Catherine described my state to him, or to any of my family members, but that grave look on his face, which I can still see today, suggests how strange and difficult a period it must have been for Catherine to manage on her own, and that I must have been an imposition on her career. After Allen left, ambling down the side of the canal and on towards the train station, I sat and looked at the water bobbing in front of me. It's sad when a sibling, whose closeness you once took as a constant in your life, detaches themselves from you, or perhaps what is sad is that you realize they have been long-detached and you have ceased to recognize in them the intensity of feeling they once generated in you. A childhood spent with siblings you care terribly for is a childhood of everyday revelations. I gazed at the patterns of light on the surface of the canal water for some time. I was entranced by three particular colours: sky blue, white-grey and extremely dark green. To the fore, near my side of the canal, the sky-blue patches, which seemed always framed within a line of white-grey, began to disintegrate, coalesce, congeal, disperse, collect, over and over again into smaller and sometimes broader blobs, pooling into each other, bobbing, bending, breaking, separating for some moments and then coming back together once again. I sat on the bench looking at this marbled region of sky blues trapped within these curves of grey-white, all above a nebulous expanse of heaving dark-green, and I recalled a section of the animated film *Fantasia*, by Disney, which I had seen with Catherine earlier that year in the Kinobar Prager in Leipzig.

I am sure I as much connect my memories of this part of the film *Fantasia* with those patterns on the surface of the water of the Royal Canal as I do both with a particular grouping of high-shouldered birds on stacks of electricity poles I used to see often, when I was a youth, on the edges of the dusky boglands on the outskirts of my hometown. I am not sure, though, if I am not simply conflating these shifting patterns and colours on the canal water with my understanding of Disney's methods of animation, and if so I am not sure if I am placing these two registers of the meaning of the word 'animation' upon the up-till-then unanimated wetlands to the outskirts of my hometown, covered over in stacks of dark poles with arrays of indifferent white lake birds perched atop, but I am sure that the part of Disney's *Fantasia* that I am remembering is the segment that was edited out of the first cinema release of the film – the segment that was called 'Moonlight', and I remember it as being of no more than three minutes in length. Its opening scene featured a conductor and then an orchestra in blue silhouette, which by the strange magic of the dissolving animator's drawings, all transformed into a swampland pool deep in the Florida Everglades being approached by a lone and timid egret. This egret then stops at the edge of this pool and stretches its wings serenely, and the furthest tip of this wing touches the surface of the pool below enough to send concentric ripples out into the hitherto stagnant water. The egret then steps along the shore before dipping its slender beak into the pool to sate some celluloid version of thirst. Then the egret wades into the water, up to its knee-height ankles, building pace with the accompanying orchestral music and sending further ripples and waves outward as it progresses. It takes flight as the music soars. It lifts clear of the water, glides through the blue Everglades, through the canopy of surrounding trees and across the glow of the full moon above, where the egret then arcs a number of times around the outline of the moon before swooping back down into the Everglades and landing gently in another pool of water, sending ripples again out across its extents. Then, as if awakening some other consciousness, a closer view of these ripples and wavelets travelling across the water appears. The music falls into a tumble of stringed thrums. The reflection of the moon settles and gathers as the excitation on the surface of the water recedes. While the music thrums again, this time louder, more waves appear and break the image of the moon back up into sparkling multitudes, over and over, into what I remember as a somewhat heart-breaking rhythm. The view of this swamp world then shifts towards the source of the new ripples – a second egret … but I did not admire the remainder of this segment of the cinematic release, or at least I did not admire its message.

On the odd occasion when I visited home in Ireland after Allen had passed away, Edel would make a point of calling me 'disconnected' and I never quite got to the pitch of what she might have meant until after her, Jo's and Louise's funerals, all three coming a year apart, in the early 2000s, when life, by this time, had become the systematic thinning-out of a church pew. By the end of it all I became a kind of mechanical animal that turned up at the chapel in B—— to shake hands and smile at a procession of strangers whose warmth and goodwill for my deceased sisters fell painfully short of me.

After Allen had wandered off to Drumcondra train station that day, and after the segment of time I spent gazing at the shifting patterns in the oily canal water came to an end, I looked up at the tree above me and spied two separate leaves flourishing from the ends of two separate branches, both leaf tips twitching in what must have been a pleasant summer's breeze, and after a while looking over and back at these leaf tips bobbing in a seemingly independent way, about two linear feet from each other, a distant airplane appeared deep in the sky blue above. It emerged, this speck of far-off aluminium, steel, plastics, flesh and oil from behind the tip of the lower leaf and it drew a perfect white line across the sky up to the higher leaf tip. Then the tube of light disappeared behind the second leaf and the body of the whole tree. The airplane's trail of exhaust, though, sat there for a few seconds measuring the disparity between the rhythms of the bobbing tips of the two leaves I'd been looking up at. White, sky blue, then bright green. I looked on until the distant line of white dissolved into the darker blue beyond and the tips of green became at once abstracted, untethered and all the more real again.

△

I SIT ON THE ARMCHAIR between the two sets of record players, amps and speakers. The drill I heard not ten minutes ago has erupted once more. Its clatter seems to come now from behind me, but from a distance away. The thudding whine rises, then falls off and is replaced by the clink of hollow metal on metal – the sounds of steel scaffolding elements meeting each other. The crumpling bangs and shouts of scaffolding being erected or taken down are the sounds I most associate with Bilbao. Looking at a building shrouded over in scaffolding is a pleasing way for me to grid-out and re-organize a façade into its constituent parts. From a distance, particularly if a building is very ornate, I find the frames scaffolding gives to a building of great use in helping me to understand what is going on over the course of the whole façade – where the patterns of interplay happen, how many times a particular flourish might appear, or the change in ratio of vertical to horizontal dimensions of windows as they ascend … Sometimes, if I have the energy, I swap frames around and begin completely to disfigure the ornamentation. There was a game I once received for Christmas from my father's mother, Nana Pura. I can remember of her only a clenched face and delicate hands, but the game she gave me is still quite clear in my mind; it was a small plastic frame within which were twenty-four smaller square pieces. One square in the five-by-five grid was missing so you could slide a square over and back or up and down, thus making room for its neighbour.

When in the correct order, the image the squares relayed was of a bouquet of red and blue flowers of a type I for some reason now associate with Eastern Europe. I was adept at this game and would spend hours mixing up the composition and sliding it back together again. This game I most often think about after gazing at a scaffolded-out building in the distance, with men walking over and back carrying out their work.

The sound of the clinking metal tubes falls away. I lift the needle onto the quintet to my left. At first it plays at too loud a volume. Then I turn it to a volume I can barely hear. I look to the wall in front of me and I listen. As the first couple of bars appear and fade, as the jolly notes and chords of the piano rise and fall, my mind fills with the substance of the photograph my brother took of me many years ago standing in between the third and fourth employee my father gave work to on his sliver of bog, us all leaning on our slanes to the fore of the soon-to-be-developed boglands on the outskirts of B——. To the left-hand edge of the image lies a dark rise in the ground and beyond this rise I recall the land there transforms into a whin-fringed swamp, and beyond that, way out of frame, runs a slim curve of dark coniferous trees, planted there one winter by the wealthy farmer whose ewe's exposed knee bone I once spied while holding the creature's head to the floor of our barn. Beyond the copse of non-indigenous coniferous trees, then, the domestic bogland extends towards the horizon in the mid-west, it another rolling swathe of land that flattens and lowers itself into further industrialized peat boglands beyond. To the foreground of this out-of-sight place, just past the curve of coniferous trees, I remember two corrugated shelters, about twenty metres apart – one tall and the other squat. One day, back when Allen and Edel and I went roaming over that part of the countryside, miles outside of town, I heard the clatter of distant gunshots. We had not heard gunshots for many years, except for Hunting Sunday, which had been brought to a halt during the Emergency and had not by then begun again in our part of the county. The distant gunshots we heard that soft day were regular and they reverberated almost welcomingly across the land. Allen, Edel and I stalked up to the curve of coniferous trees, thinking that we might be able to discern what was happening on the other side by peeking through any gaps available in the foliage. I stepped into the curve of evergreens taking care not to tread on a twig or anything that might draw attention to what I assumed then would be an unwanted approach. The gunshots emanated from one of the two corrugated structures, but I could not tell which one or why. I was a timid child and I am surprised I continued on through the dense curve of evergreens to see what was occurring. By this time Allen and Edel had fled back home, scared by the sounds on the other side. I pushed through some branches, then looked on for some time until I realized the gunshots were coming from the elevated structure. I could not at first tell what was going on in the lower structure other than that a person was in there operating some sort of spring-loaded tool. Then, the person in the taller structure called a word abruptly to the person I could partially see in the lower structure and something appeared in the sky, like a bird, hurled by this machine. The object curved into the sky, up and away from the lower structure sitting to the right of the taller structure. I followed the object for a moment or two; then, BANG! – it disappeared. Later that evening when I spoke to my father about this, he told me that the man conducting the practice was one who'd recently moved to town as a senior clerk with the speedily expanding electrification scheme. I stood under the cover of the sapping evergreens, looking on in awe, until the place began to darken. They must have shot another fifty times: 'Pull,' beautiful arc, BANG, obliteration, smoke plumes from the taller structure; 'pull,' beautiful arc, BANG, beautiful arc continues to the ground in the far distance, smoke plumes from the taller structure; 'pull,' beautiful arc, BANG, small deflection of the arc, smoke plumes from the taller structure; 'pull,' beautiful arc, BANG, obliteration, smoke plumes from the taller structure; 'pull,' beautiful arc, BANG, obliteration, smoke plumes from the taller structure … until eventually, like a skipped beat, the word 'pull' didn't occur. Instead the person in the taller structure stepped down a ladder leaning to the left-hand side of the trussed legs and he walked over to the smaller structure where the man I struggled to make out emerged. The man from the taller structure, a large bald person, had his gun barrel broken over his forearm as he and his slightly built blond-haired companion walked directly towards me laughing and chatting. I, standing stock still, noted the faces of the men and promised myself I'd talk to them about this pastime of theirs at the next chance I had. I never did. Children then didn't begin conversations with adults. Even though it had become quite dark, I stole out from the edge of the curve of coniferous trees and made my way towards the two structures. I looked into the smaller structure and saw the armature for flinging the objects I'd seen arcing beautifully across the sky a few minutes earlier. Scattered around the machine were shards of a lurid-yellow-and-black ceramic. I leaned in, picked

133

up a fragment and turned it over in my hand; then, for fear of being accused of stealing I flung it back in. It clapped dryly on the floor. I climbed the metal ladder leaning against the legs of the taller corrugated structure and pulled myself into this simple chamber. It had a broad rectangular window-opening to the front, while on the damp and rusted floor lay scattered scores of spent red shotgun cartridges. I surveyed the dark and wet land beyond. It was rare on land so flat for me to see it from this kind of elevation. I felt exalted. Peering down to my right I imagined a clay pigeon flying out from the darkness of the smaller structure and curving up into an arc in the sky. I raised an imaginary shotgun to my shoulder, but I did not have the heart to interrupt the flight of that imaginary clay pigeon as it arced and fell. I looked to the dark bogland beyond to measure the point where it might have landed. After some time, watching imaginary clay pigeons whizzing out from the dark below, I pulled the trigger of my imaginary gun and visualized a successful shot and the clay pigeon bursting into smithereens and raining down in a shower of lurid-yellow-and-black ceramic fragments. I did it again, and again, this time giving the armature flinging my clay pigeons incredible strength, and I pictured these things flying far far higher in the sky each time and me either obliterating them mid-curve or missing them, or not firing at them at all and allowing them to complete their once-exorbitant arcs to the ground. By this stage it was quite dusky, but I, excited by this place, did not care. I descended from the creaking elevated structure and walked out into the black bogland with water soaking onto my feet, until I came upon a daisy-ring of lurid-yellow-and-black ceramic fragments. I looked back towards the two structures, then I looked directly above the daisy ring and I drew in the sky a large curved triangle with the point of obliteration above me as the apex of this three-sided form.

I LOOK TO MY HANDS folded over in my lap and can hear Schubert's distant music still rise and fall and release. When my fingernails grow to what would be considered a normal length, my hands begin to remind me of my father's. I look from my hands to the naked white wall in front of me and I visualize once again this squat bog triangle in the sky of my mind's eye, but I have come out from underneath and the triangle has transformed into the shape it would take if I were behind it and looking on from the edge of the curve of coniferous trees to the rear of the two corrugated structures. I see a taller triangular shape, its apex in the cloud-grey sky and two base points connecting the small and taller structures below. I imagine the form this shape would take if I were to draw the converging arcs of the exploding spray of shotgun pellets and the clay pigeon, but in this instance I imagine the objects miss each other mid-air and I allow them to complete their crossing arcs down to their separate resting places on the bogland below. I then realize, sitting in my chair visualizing these two arcs crossing each other in the flatland sky, that I have drawn this form before on one of the acetate sheets I, in the evenings, sometimes place over my brother's photograph of my father's four workmen and me; so I stand, remove the needle from the record, walk to the bottom drawer of my desk and take out my slim plywood box containing these drawings.

I walk to the kitchen and notice still some gentle shafts of the reflected morning sun are meeting the walls. I lift from the section of wall to the right of the window I'd gazed out of not half an hour ago the aluminium-and-glass framed photograph my brother once took, and I slip it from its casing.

I return to my desk in the sitting room and lay the photograph beside the stack of acetate drawings and begin, drawing by drawing, to place a sheet of acetate over my brother's ancient photograph until I find what it is I am looking for – those crossing arcs in miniature appearing and disappearing behind the small rise in the land towards the left-hand edge of the image.

I stand at my desk, looking down at this historic form.

'Hm,' I say.

Towards the background of the photograph I place myself high up in the space in the sky where the arcs of a clay pigeon and a poorly shot cluster of pellets slide past each other and, looking around from this imagined position, I piece together what is left on the land. In the distance below lies my father's sliver of bog, then, beyond, a line of poles holding two drooping lines of cables, running alongside the canal that bisects the low-lying single street of B——, with more rolling hills and farmland unfurling into the distance, all scattered with white-walled cottages issuing thin blue strings of smoke from their chimneys, and fields edged out with dense rectilinear hedges demarcating an array of townlands with three-, four- and five-syllable names: Derrynagalliagh, Derrynaskea, Derrymore, Derrymany, Derryneel. A silent murmuration of starlings casts up from a stand of sycamore extending out across the hinterlands.

The birds sweep to the left. To the right, though, I see nothing but an encroaching darkness. I swing back through to what remains, past the water tower and forlorn church spires, the line of poles that runs up alongside the canal and past the bog that edges the town and the plains of pre-industrialized bogland below until I face west where the murmuration of starlings sweeps back down, dispersing and settling like falling tea leaves onto another stand of broad sycamores in the distance. Then, looking beyond the farthest end of the slight rise in the land, I see the yellow-beige model substation and pylon. To the rear of the substation I see the excitable young man stiff as a pole, he still toppling over and over while relaying the troubled journey of an ocean-going steamer delivering skinned Finnish trees to Limerick Port; and I remember, while standing here in my apartment in Bilbao, looking on at the tall crossing arcs in the sky to the left-hand edge of my brother's photograph, what this excitable young man said when he eventually stopped laughing at the good of himself and sat back down alongside me. Having leafed through to the end of the publication he was still grasping, he told me that before anything of the electrification scheme was possible that the State had sent an Irish forester to northern Finland, in advance of purchasing the trees they would use as electricity poles, to ensure that the Finns had enough of the right size of tree for the scheme's use, and that before the State handed over millions of pounds for these trees, they wanted to make sure the Finns 'were not pulling the wool over their eyes'. I remember the excitable young man reading to me, from the back of the publication, extracts of letters the young forester had sent back to HQ in Ireland – they were written in the style of a penny thriller and this, as I sat back then on the edge of an expanse of bog, and as I stand now gazing down at the tall crossing arcs to the left-hand edge of my brother's photograph, triggered then, and triggers now views onto further landscapes, land-scapes of the Finnish countryside covered in snow with multitudes of vertical black lines in forest-like arrangements laid upon it.

I picture that Irish forester in rural Finland, dres-sed in dark fur-lined clothing, on the edge of a vast white frigid lake fringed and cleaved with these tree-sized vertical black lines. He looks out over the land as his breath plumes before him. In the distance, towards the seeming middle of the frozen-over lake, lies an island, and the young forester with timber skis fastened to his feet, and with ski-sticks in his gloved hands, makes off onto this lake. He pulls a timber sled behind him, it tied to his waist with a length of pale rope. The sled, which is similar in shape to a small boat, is full of provisions – a tent, his measuring equipment and some tinned rations. The young forester makes off as it begins to snow, inscribing a long smooth line into the virgin drifts as he goes. He passes through a thicket of vertical black lines to the other side of the island where in the distance he spies another larger island, one he believes to hold a more bountiful selection of suitable timber, so he rights his hat and reties his rope to his waist and makes off for the island in the distance. He builds a rhythm: left foot, right foot, left ski, right ski, they appearing below him on the snow, sinking an inch or two into the fresh crystals as he proceeds, metre by metre, across the expanses to the next island, whereupon, noticing that the light has fallen into a strange fabric of dark, he sets up camp, eats and by carbide torchlight describes his progress – in the first of many letters to be sent back to the electrification-office HQ for publication, letters that will find themselves read aloud one day by an excitable young man sitting on some poles to the rear of a substation adjacent to a Midlands' bog. The forester falls asleep in his tent in the midst of a circular arrangement of vertical black lines. That night, in the sky over his tiny camp, a multitude of silent fireworks from unknown sources explode, shower and explode again in spasms of colour and light illuminating the magnitudes of dark and white around him.

Next morning the forester stumbles from his tent, relieves himself, straightens, pushes a handful of snow into his mouth and, in the improved conditions, spies yet another island in the distance and beyond that an incline. The land otherwise is utterly flat, a wilderness of quaking white planes propped and interpenetrated by vertical black lines. He pushes off with the hope of making by sundown the foothills of the incline. It is snowing heavily but this forester continues onward, head bowed, his breath blooming again out before him. He visualizes the backs of his skis and the two lines in the snow emanating from him, them being covered over again by the underside of the boat-like sled he tugs, its tiny stern listing across the miniature mounds and dips in this terrain of white. A broad line of snow appears from the rear of the sled and the small ring attached to the stern sends tiny dings out across the vastness. His ski sticks, lifting and falling either side of this line, plot a staggered arrangement of sunken circles into the snow, as if two single-footed mechanical birds were hopping alongside him as he goes, guiding him on his way.

Beyond the last island of vertical black lines he sees the incline, covered in snow and mist, and he notices that the vertical black lines gathered in the foothills morph into triangles of dark-green conifers as they scatter around the exposed rocky outcrops at the summit, and I realize – looking on at this forester looking on at this outcrop – that it is from the cover of the Eterna Edition record featuring that reproduction of the painting of Friedrich's *Morning Mist in the Mountains*, and I recall now, standing over my desk looking at the arcs-on-acetate placed over my brother's photograph, of a day, a year or so after Catherine and I had purchased the record, when Catherine, looking over my shoulder, uttered quietly to me, 'That reproduction's the wrong way around.' I looked to her then, and she told me that the reproduction had been flipped around the vertical axis, because in the painting – which she'd seen earlier that year in Dresden – the outcrop points to the right-hand side of the edge of the original, whereas on the record sleeve it is pointed to the left. I push away from my desk, walk back to the record player and pick up the sleeve and, because I have never seen the painting in the flesh, I can only assume that it is the mirror image of what I am looking at now and that this reproduction of Friedrich's painting is placing me behind the wall upon which Friedrich's painting now hangs, wherever that may be, and this reproduction, whether I know it truly or not, has always put me into this dark place behind what Friedrich had in his mind's eye. I remember Catherine despising his viewpoint anyway, she claiming this elevated view of the top of this snow-and-mist-enswirled mountain was inhumane, because of its lack of depicted foreground. The implication being, she said, that it placed the artist into the heavens, where what was sublime in the experience of the mountain – the view, for instance, that the young Irish forester may have received down on the plains of snow below – was extinguished. She despised the painter's view here because she claimed it was an economist's view of the land, but an economist feigning delight at nature, because, she always claimed, if from this same position the painter looked directly downward, the viewpoint would be of land, flattened, and prepared for mapping and proportioning and organizing in a manner that removed the person making the proportioning and organizing from the voices of those on the land below – both the economist and the painter in this position were out of earshot, she claimed. I consider this reverse image for a while longer and think Catherine perhaps was on to something, seeing Romantic-era view-making as consonant with the economic view-making of land and life below – and that all the land-surveying equipment of this time took its technology from gun sights was not lost on Catherine either; it was a connection she pointed out to me happily. Her thought reverberates like a

143

gunshot into the counterclockwise-swirling morning mists of this image before me now.

I return to the desk holding the acetate drawing placed over my brother's photograph. Though I am not looking at the forester any longer, I can imagine, through a phantom wetness in the seat of my pants, my youthful self sitting on the wet lengths of dark Finnish timber to the rear of the German substation, looking onto the Irish bog, listening to this excitable young man who recounts these letters from the forester in Finland. The excitable young man describes the forester's walk up the incline, and he tells me that as night falls a spot of light appears magically overhead illuminating this forester's route and throwing the trees around him into ghastly shadows. The forester, according to his dispatches, does not stop – he proceeds through the thickening blizzard into a world of blue-black as the mounds of snow gather around him, until the trees too, nearby, become mummified and are rendered completely white. The snow heaps and gathers up onto the trees as the forester struggles past, until the trees themselves cease to look like trees and begin to resemble curved globular statues of shining marble, and I, as a young boy sitting listening to this excitable young man recounting the forester's experience, begin to see what my younger self would have seen had he

leaned forward in the rain that day when he encountered the porcelain electricity insulator in its grassy
grave and picked up the shiny node and felt its heft
for himself – I see an all-encompassing flash of white.

I'M BREATHING HEAVILY NOW. I sit down in my armchair once again. It creaks as I recline; then the room
is silent. My stomach gurgles. I cough, inhale, swal-
low and cough once more. I return my stare to the
near-naked living-room wall before me. I no longer
have my younger self sitting alongside the excitable
young man in mind, but I, on my own, am now curious to follow the route the forester has made over
this blanched Scandinavian corner of Finland.

I see the forester meeting a fisherman in the middle of an empty plain of snow a few days before the
tired forester runs out of provisions. This forester
pulls from his pocket a map, which is without feature,
and he asks the fisherman to indicate where he is and
where it is he should go to find the stocks of timber he
needs for electricity poles back in Ireland. The fisherman opens the map out onto the snow and points
to where the reserves of timber in this part of the
world are stored – in the middle of the top right-hand
quadrant of the map; and he then indicates where the
forester currently stands – a point in the snow about

a foot to the right of the very top right-hand corner of the folded-out sheet of linen-backed mapping paper. The forester asks the fisherman if he can bring him south west to the timber. The tall and ruddy-faced fisherman, after looking over the forester's shoulder for some time – taking in the white land beyond and a vast encroaching triangular-shaped darkness above, a kite-darkness that the forester seems to have hauled along at a great distance behind him – looks back into the face of the forester and, once reading the great need in the forester's features, nods, returns to his fishing hole, pulls his fishing line up out of the deep circle of ice that leads to the sky blues beneath, rolls the line up into a ball and points the forester to his sled. The forester uncouples himself from his own now near-empty sled, ties it to the rear of the fisherman's larger sled, climbs in, covers himself over with sealskins and begins to nod off … only waking at intervals as the land around him slides by, altering incrementally from total white to white-sky blue to grey-white to green, and he knows with the appearance of this dark green that he has arrived at the stock of material he must somehow organize for delivery back to Ireland for its systematic rearrangement as poles thrust into the countryside.

I STAND. My breathing has calmed. I see shadows and sunlight. I walk to my desk and look up at the edge of the image of the Alpine mountain peaks on the front of the Italian postcard, but the image has softened. I blink. I look down and push my brother's photograph and the acetate sheets lying across it to one side, slide my desk drawer out, pull my usually unused notebook from it and open the notebook out on the table.

Then, I begin to draw across a two-page spread, with a cracked and rather dirty Staedler stencil, a row of four circles.

Within each circle I am carefully writing out certain words or groupings of words in neat lettering, referring to entities of equal prominence and seeming-value that have emerged to me this morning, and they are: Schubert, Walser's '4', Allen's photograph, Serra's steel sculptures.

As I look at these circles it then occurs to me that the best way to show the secondary entities that have arrived to me this morning would be to draw a random loop of smaller circles around the four larger circles in the central band of the notebook. And into these smaller circles I write further words and word/ number groupings denoting these secondary things.

ON THE DOUBLE-PAGE SPREAD before me now I count, all in, forty-three circles. Criss-crossing somewhat complicatedly between these many entities are blue lines connecting them in a manner where the connection is apparent in the first degree. The blue lines between the circles seem to mass together at points, then fall away into framed-out and almost derelict absences. Once I had completed the action of drawing each connecting line, the direction of the thought collapsed into a two-way channel, and the once-order of my actual thoughts broke down. All I am left with is this diagram showing a complicated stillness of mind. And in this diagram there appears, at first glance, to be at least four striking features:

—Most of the lines in the drawing emanate from or lead to a small circle near the top right-hand corner of the pages with the word 'Catherine' in it.

—The circle to the centre left with the word 'Sabbatical' in it has no line of connection to or from it.

—Though the words 'Serra's Steel Sculpture' is one of the four major circles in the central band of the page, it only has one line of connection and that leads down to the circle with the words 'Walser's Skull' written in it.

149

—The circle with the words 'Young Danish Engineer' in it is surrounded by three other circles containing the words: 'Office in Leipzig', 'Ammonia Plotter' and 'Tracing Paper'. And from this cluster runs a line from the circle holding the words 'Young Danish Engineer' directly to the circle with the words 'Indian Bridges' resting in it, and this circle then triangulates with two other circles below, with the words 'Living Root Bridges' and 'Last Notebook' in them. From here, and I find this fascinating because I can't remember quite which germinated which, this unwieldy cluster then leads down to a small circle near the bottom left of the page holding the words 'Table-Tennis Bats' in it, which in turn produces three prongs, one to a circle containing the words 'Praktica Camera', one back to the circle with 'Catherine' in it and one on to a circle containing the name 'Edel', which then leads to the circle hosting 'Sheep's Knee Bone', which leads then onto two circles, one with the words 'Jo's Sputum' and the other with the word 'Porcelain'. This leads on to 'Grassi Museum' and that arrows back across the whole interface to a circle on the verso side of the notebook with the word 'Leipzig' lying in it, which leads on to 'Office in Leipzig', which then, finally, runs back to the beginning of this route, to the circle containing the words 'Young Danish Engineer'.

This one circulation then produces a few larger questions: If I were to add to this diagram another produced at this time tomorrow, and if I were to compare them, could I then deduce from these changing forms a changing of mind? An enriching of mind? Or a deterioration of mind?

Turning the notebook drawing about in front of me, I then consider what would happen if I were to re-fashion these circles as spheres. Perhaps someday I could ask a young child who can expertly blow soap bubbles to blow one for me, but without releasing it from the plastic stem. Then, raising the underside of the partly blown bubble, straddling the oval of the plastic stem, this child could blow once more into the wobbling shining chamber of the first bubble and graft onto its side another bubble segment, and perhaps onto the side of that yet another bubble, and onto that another, and another and another, et cetera. Perhaps if I could find an expert enough child to do this, he or she could then blow this whole formation of forty-three interconnecting bubble-ettes out, and if that were possible then surely I could ask an expert glass blower to blow this whole form for me; then when it casts and cools, I could take this bulbous thing in my hands and hold it up to the midday light, turn it about and inspect the form and its many imperfections. Then, if it was a sunny day, I could carry this glassy orb-thing to a wall and rotate it in direct sunlight while inspecting the shadows it projects onto the wall and from there re-consider the variety of tones and shapes and interconnections and interpenetrations, and as I might rotate in my hands in the midday sun this form, with its shadows rotating in tones and smudges upon the wall before me, I could at least then say: 'Today, my thoughts might well look like this.'

I turn the page of the notebook and draw a large circle in the middle of it and write the word 'Catherine' through the centre. Then I turn the next page over and I draw out four large circles again in the middle third of the page, each circle about an inch in diameter and each about an inch apart, and I write the words, 'Edel', 'Jo', 'Allen' and 'Louise' into them. Then I take out my ruler and the blue pencil I had used to interconnect the circles on the pages previous and I draw a horizontal line across the page starting from the left-hand edge, through all four circles and each name in the centre of each circle and continue the line out past the right-hand edge of the page. Then I put the pencil down, fold over the notebook and put it back into my drawer. Then I walk over to the balcony doors and step out into the morning air.

TO MY LEFT, down the syncline of Solokoetxe, the morning traffic is hooting and bicycle bells dring. From here I can see the junction where my street meets the old town's Kalea Ronda and the Plaza Santos Juanes, and just beyond, through the slim corridor of buildings, the soft sandstone dome of the Church of Saint Antony breaches the sky. Beyond that again, the city, the body of which I don't know so well, rises, then becomes mountain covered over in trees, and beyond the mountain ridge lie valleys and plains that I will most likely not ever see.

Today will be warm, though, I can tell by the haze on the hills. I can smell the river too, and what is in it of the sea.

THE RAILING on my balcony is a well-turned wrought-iron thing painted a green so dark that from a distance one might think it black. From over the edge of the railing I have hung three grey plastic flowerpots containing three red geraniums. These flowers are thriving because I water them lightly every second day. I remember to water the geraniums whenever I have taken my coffee from the pewter cup. After I finish my coffee in the kitchen I fill a milk jug with water and come out here and water the flowers, then look a while up and down the road to see who is out and if I recognize them. Strangers pass. There is enough room to unfold a small chair and table on this balcony, but I prefer to simply stand here for a few minutes each morning and look out. I have not owned a balcony before and I take some pleasure still from standing out here and looking around.

To the right, on the street below my balcony, run two rows of six sycamore trees sheltering a single bench. Four old streetlights stand at either end, their heads disappearing up into rustling foliage. In the summer evenings when I sit there, having returned from my day, I watch the shifting leaf-shadows bathe in the pools of sodium-coloured light around me.

A group of young chattering workmen in dark T-shirts and dust-white work pants have gathered down there now and they are leaning against the wall on this side of the sycamore trees. They have coffees in their hands. These men will soon remove the many pieces of scaffolding mounded in their trucks parked a little further up Solokoexte and no doubt clang an arrangement of scaffolding around the building next door.

Back to my left, the road turns up into Kalea Sorkunda, which is a street on an incline that leads on to a park and beyond to the church hospital. One day, soon after I settled here, I wandered a few hundred yards up the Sorkunda and came upon a music school, it a substantial two-storey building fronting onto the narrow carriageway. That morning, as I passed underneath an open window, I could hear a tuba and a clarinet playing some sort of duet. The two students playing these instruments were obviously getting to know the music, because every now and then the tune would break down, they'd mutter something to each other, then some moments later start up again and play for a while, then break down, then they played uninterruptedly for almost two whole minutes. I leaned back against the wall as the music poured out over my head and I realized I was enjoying this music because it lacked mastery, and this lack of mastery contained for me drama and tension that seemed to colour deeply what I could possibly sense around me at that time. A dog began barking farther up the hill, a bell pealed from the church, a truck rattled past and on a small pitched roof to the top of a building back down the street two men, who'd clambered off a tower of scaffolding a few moments before, began scorching bitumen onto the roof felt with a flamethrower. I looked at the younger of the two roofers. He was without a safety harness and he stood with what I thought was a disproportionate calmness on the edge of the roof – the blue-red flame arrowing out in front of him, and I imagined him slipping and falling to the ground and the flame spinning in the air. Then the music broke down into parps and peeps once more. As I wandered down the hill the music then gathered stertorously back up again behind me, and as I returned past the scaffolding the roofers had clambered from, I thought of a pastel work I saw in the Grassi on the evening of Catherine's retirement. The work was called *The Chocolate Girl* and had been composed by a French artist called Liotard. That part of the gallery that evening was quiet, and all I could think about while gazing at the pale pastel granules making up this image of a young lady dressed in a pink-and-white bonnet and dark frock – she carrying a cup of chocolate and a tall glass of water on a tray from left to right across the frame of the image – was the description of entropy in the Second Law of Thermodynamics. I thought then if this image were to disintegrate and if the coloured grains of pastel were carried off, dispersing and gathering and dispersing and gathering in giant vectoring winds across the entropic cosmos, to some alien interface similar in size and material to the one holding the grains of pastel I looked at that day in the Grassi, arranged so expertly by this Liotard almost 300 years before, and if these same grains were to land on this interface in this far distant place in exactly the form with which they were arranged before me then, then it would be in front of this second version of this handsome pastel work that I would find Catherine, she gazing and probably contemplating, like me, on how such a work could possibly come into being.

After I leave my place today, I will wander all the way down Solokoetxe, almost to where it meets the river, and turn right onto the end of La Ronda, where this small café I frequent called La Gernikesa sits alongside a tobacco shop, and it is at this café that I will sip my last coffee of the day. There is a wooden bench to the front of the café and I sit here most days from just before nine to up on nearly eleven. If the weather is very warm I might sit there until twelve, watching the sun slide around the busy corner. People go past, usually people as old as me, and sometimes older, and we nod to each other. Some of them, who enter for a morning coffee or a beer, often give me a smile and a thumbs-up. A lady I see each day leaves her cigar on a notch carved out of the ledge beside me as she steps in for her coffee. The smell of the cigar is pleasant, though I have no interest in smoking it myself. Most days I am joined by a man called Jorge, who must be only in his early sixties, but who cannot talk. He has a hole in his throat on account of a poorly executed procedure for throat cancer, I suspect, a procedure carried out, I suspect, in the hospital back up at the top of the hill overlooking the city. He wrote his name out for me one morning on a slip of paper he'd taken from his pocket. It was crumpled and covered over in words and I thought that this must be how he communicates with those who don't understand his sign language. We sit together on this bench each day for a while and wordlessly point out strange and/or amusing and/or incidental things happening on the street before us. And Jorge, a large man, with black hair and what would be called a sickly pallor, either grunts or smiles or chuckles. Up to the hour of nine o'clock, especially on weekdays, the corner becomes its most busy and its most affectionate. Schoolchildren with their parents descend Solokoexte or emerge from La Ronda, or up from the La Ribera to the right, and they all gather at the traffic lights. Here children of a certain age are kissed goodbye, or younger children are brought by the hand across the street to the primary school on the other side of the river. You can see the beginnings of friendships at this junction, shy waves out from between the legs of parents and the first looks of what might become confidence between friends. I feel sometimes like I am witnessing the beginnings of types of trust that will last lifetimes. Then these people swarm over and disappear around the rear of the church until another coagulation of children and parents gathers up around the lights. These people loiter for a while, then surge across the carriageway again.

THE YOUNG SCAFFOLDERS below me are laughing at something one of the older scaffolders must have said. He is a broad-shouldered man who has smoked furiously since he has arrived. His arms are now spread out wide. He lifts his left elbow, pointing it upward, and he churns his downward-pointing hand in circles, all the while laughing with his audience. I look from them to my flowers and see that some of the leaves of my geranium on the left-hand side are drying out. I once used to pick the dead leaves off the geraniums so as to allow, at least in my mind, a greater and more direct flow of nutrients and water towards the petals that were already flourishing or those that were still in bud or were about to flourish. Then one day, while removing some withered petals, I looked to the building across the way and a woman of an age similar to mine was shaking her head. She

159

also had geraniums, of many different and vibrant colours, and she said something back across the way to me, in Basque, about the care of flowers. Then, registering my look of incomprehension, she simply shook her finger and indicated with the sort of hand-movements I have come to understand of people here, that the flowers did not need to be helped with their flourishing in this way – that these sorts of flowers will bloom and prosper on their own. I am not entirely sure if this is what she was indicating, but I have stopped picking off the dead petals and I think this has led to my small grouping of geraniums doing well. I have come to realize also that a cluster of dead or dying petals nearby to a cluster of healthy petals has the interesting effect of drawing and giving beauty to both.

The scaffolders on the street below are finishing up their coffees and have begun to unload their planks and metal tubes. They place them in neat stacks, and in some cases lean them in clusters across from the wall they will soon be covering over. I can tell by the thinness of the tubing that this scaffolding will only be used for access to the façade or more likely to the roof; the scaffolding will not be required to hold materials or large tools. One of the men slides out a hook-and-wheel pulley and drops it on the ground beside a craggy mound of metal corner-clamps. As the pulley smacks the paving stones, like sparks from a flint, scores of images of the line of a tower-crane's boom drawn across a forgotten sky gush to mind. The boom in each image splits the sky in two, and the colours of the sky either side of this line of steel alternates from pink-blue, to blue-pink, to red-blue, to red-pink, to pink-blue and over again, a sort of repeating pattern of blocks of colour separated by this trussed-up line, the whole image like a fragment of stained glass taken from a far larger dome of stained glass. I remember clambering up a tower crane at dawn one winter morning to look out over the dark peaks and plateaus of the city of Leipzig. I wanted to see the sky beyond the alternating colours either side of the line of the truss that had up till then interrupted my view onto the heavens. People were shouting at me from the street below and I am sure I acknowledged them from the sky-filled background of pink and then the background of blue and then the background of red, and I am sure I felt unwell and dizzy up there. I am bound to have. And I am also sure that it was a very cold day and that the steel triangles of the swaying tower-crane's boom were wet and frigid and slippery and that my hands, when I eventually made it back to the ground again, were corpse-white with a lack of circulation. I recall a blanket being put over my shoulders by a carpenter's apprentice. He

161

was dressed in a dusty black top hat and cloak, and he helped me to lie down. I consider what it is I have not been told and what I can't remember and what I will not ever know about this period in Leipzig, and it amounts to near void.

I look from the pulley on the ground to the window belonging to the lady who once advised me on how best to care for my geraniums, but she does not appear. A shout comes from the street below. It is a woman I do not recognize, until she smiles and waves again and calls: 'Hola!' to which I reply: 'Hola,' too.

I once saw in an old magazine sepia photographs of an indigenous Bolivian family standing around a fire on the edge of a forest. This woman reminds me of the girls of this family; so I would guess her to be of Bolivian extraction. Some evenings when I am walking the last few yards back up towards my apartment, this woman appears beside me, and she takes my hand in hers until we reach the bench beneath the sycamore trees where I usually catch my breath before going inside. She leads me to the bench then stands over me, her palm placed on my shoulder until my breathing has steadied; then she nods and leaves and rounds the corner up towards Kalea Sorkunde. She is a large woman, and she usually carries shopping bags full of groceries over her shoulders, and I imagine her later each evening feeding a large quantity of people in a noisy room elsewhere in the city. I have never seen her from this elevation before, so I begin to laugh at the oddness of seeing this kind woman, in the morning light, from this height, and she, who has possibly never seen me from such a depth before, begins also to laugh, and maybe she, seeing me finding this scenario so surprising and so funny, allows my mirth to add to hers, and we are now laughing and nodding and waving at each other. Then she waves once more, still laughing, and moves off, making for where the street narrows and descends to the junction of Solokoetxe and Kalea Ronda, where I imagine the shutters of La Gernikesa café are being rattled up, and the owner, a tall, balding and at times poor-tempered man in his early sixties, is preparing for his day of business while looking out onto the street he will step into a few moments hence to bid a good morning, I imagine, to the lady in the tobacco shop next door.

 ↻

THE AFTERNOON I first flew into Bilbao, as the airplane veered around the nub of land where the Bay of Biscay runs from southern France into northern

Spain, an accumulation of cloud way off to my left bulged up into a distant field of white. Up till then I was feeling empty and unsure about leaving Leipzig. As the airplane descended, the whiteness around me rose. It had been a wet and cold day, but up in the sky above the clouds rumbling over the city it was brilliant and sunny. As we eased down, the distant tip of a southern mountain protruded upward into the otherwise flat plains of white. As the mountain rose I looked on at the disappearing cloud-hill in the white-and-blue distance. Then, instances later, the city appeared below, it all tropical-lush, dark and wet. It's this downward movement, from one world to another, that I recalled the first time I stood in the centre of my favourite bridge in Bilbao – the Puente del Ayuntamiento.

I'd imagine most people who live in Bilbao and most visitors to Bilbao hold this bridge in no greater esteem than any of the other bridges. It spans across the river where the river's course veers from the south west to the north west. For the first year or so here I used to approach the bridge from the left, then I'd zigzag back over the next bridge downstream, the white skeletal Zubizuri, and on to the museum. But I can't bear to traverse the Zubizuri bridge any-more because I have grown to dislike its design and how it shakes and shivers in the wind. So these days

I approach the Puente del Ayuntamiento from the Old Town side. My first view of the bridge however was from the opposite bank, and it is from here its underside first appeared to me. Its three main girders, I believed then, were continuous things running from one bank to the other. Criss-crossing in the shadows below these girders were slim lines of bracing that run over and back to the stone piers resting deep in the banks of the river – piers that are covered over with handsome white granite. The bridge bears a broad carriageway of tarmacadam and two concrete footpaths. The ramparts and handrails on the flanks of the footpaths are of well-polished steel, with delicate arched forms running between each baluster, and dotted along these edges are eight five-lanterned street lamps similar in curling ornateness and scale to those dotting out the Puenta del Arenal upstream. From the left-hand side, there is a stone tower with a small cupola roof, and passing below the carriageway runs a perpendicular underpass that continues to the promenade – Paseo Ripa – which leads on to the Paseo Uribitarte beyond. This underpass on very warm days is where I stand for a while and lean on the cool octagonal columns that dot out the umbrage. What I like most about this bridge, though, is that it fooled me. I was convinced it was a continuous structure consisting of the three steel girders underneath, until the day I walked across it and noticed at its centre that the hand-rails stop and start. There is a structural break in the middle of the bridge – a movement joint across the carriageway, splitting the structure in two. The break is filled with rubber, so it is not possible to see through the structure, but the fissure is there, and once you realize it, the nature of the bridge changes. It goes from being an arch to two broad cantilevers extending up to an absence. On warm days and when the bridge expands the gap is tiny and the rubber compresses, but on cold days the gap opens by a few millimetres and the rubber relents. You realize when you stand on and watch this bridge over a long period of time that what you are observing is closer to two lungs that merely happen to be made of building materials. If, while standing on the footpath at mid-span, you place a foot either side of the gap below and wait for a large vehicle to roll by you will feel the two ends of the bridge nod to each other, as if one hand is passing off to the other the thing traversing. What you feel up through your body is a clear tectonic tremor that repeats as each lorry or car passes, and these tremors as you walk back towards either end of the bridge die away. The silencing of these tremors is the answer the bridge is giving to the question of what it is being asked to do. The materials in the bridge are allowed to speak about their nature through their form. This is my favourite part of the bridge, walking back along it to the safety of the shore-side and feeling the bridge bringing these tremors into silence.

THESE DAYS my somewhat troubled years in Leipzig appear most often to me as a hole in the distance, but as this hole recedes from me, it grows in distinction. It becomes more lucidly a hole. What also grows in distinction, though, is the material framing out the absence, the landscapes that lead up to it, and it occurs to me that the absence is of almost no importance anymore compared to the lands of the living that surround it. I've less and less interest in pursuing the actualities of what this hole might be or even of what the material of the landscapes around it consist – I am only now concerned with the daydreams and flickering images and moods that rise up and visit me from these lands each morning.

THE SCAFFOLDERS have descended their half-built frame and are drifting off down the street for their mid-morning break. I'll take advantage of the silence to sit and listen to my two pieces of music. I return inside and sit in my armchair between my two record players and put the records on.

The two records spin slowly through the static crackle of the outer rim of each recording. The experimental symphony is on the player to my right and the quintet is still to my left. I am looking at the white wall in front of me awaiting the opening bars.

The first effort is terribly out of sync. I had misjudged the depth of the studio-silence static on each record. The experimental symphony has about a millimetre more silence. I try again, and the music starts almost in line, so I sit and listen afresh. It is not at all pleasant to listen to. It seems even at the slightest variation that the dissonance is huge and obliterating to both pieces of music. I try once more, but the recordings do not begin at the same moment, so I put my finger along the edge of the record to my right to slow it down so it will come into time with the left-hand record. I release my finger from the edge of the record when I hear both recordings reach the top of the second piano allegro, and off they go. I soon realize that the quintet has been played at a slightly slower rhythm than the experimental symphony. I am somewhat disheartened.

I try once more to play the records, this time purposefully out of sync, and this at times generates large dissonances but also moments of strange consonance.

The moments of consonance are pleasing because they draw attention to elements within the music that I had not noticed before. I had not taken great notice, for example, of the difference between the inward and outward movement of the bow along the strings of the cello. I had only previously taken notice of how the violin and cello and double bass interchanged. Then these moments of consonance disappear and I am plunged back into a dissonance again. I try turning the volume down on one, then the other, then both, until I can barely hear them at all.

I try once more to line up the two pieces of music and this time they begin a fraction out of sync, but I realize that I may as well listen to them through, seeing as I have gone to all of this trouble, so I sit back and tune in to the thirteen minutes or there-abouts (or, twenty-six minutes or thereabouts) that comprise the duration of these pieces of music. Over the course of this time the melodic elements that make up the musical work come into close proxim-ity often, then one overtakes the other, then the one that seems to have chased ahead is brought back into line and it is then gently overtaken, and the patterns of the music appear in double, like echoes, but from expansive valleys on either side of a mountain ridge. It is the moments when the overtaking happens that the two pieces of music fall briefly into synchrony.

There are moments then of good consonance, and in these moments, particularly if they coincide with any low notes in the double bass or cello, it seems for an instant as if the note is being drawn down even lower, into some other up-till-then unimaginable register beneath the surface of what I believed was the lowest note, and there this new note lies for a moment, oscillating, like a ball-bearing in the bottom of a bowl, until this sub-note is lifted back up and out into the real world of the two pieces of music progressing separately to their ends. When the sections of piano fully coincide, which is very rare, all that becomes apparent is that the two pianos used in the two pieces of music are of such different tone as to render their being placed together in this way as near irrelevant. I stand up at one point during the performance and walk away from the chair and the two sets of record players, amps and speakers, and I look back at the empty chair and the arrangement of instruments before me with the two black records, shaped now like ellipses, leading the two needles centre-ward, in broad spirals, to another crackling silence. The sound of the music from where I stand is very different. It is as if the pieces of music are being played for someone else and I have walked in on this scenario. Then I sit again. I turn the volume down on both and listen to the last four or so minutes of the two works. Their sounds appear just within the range of my hearing, and these tiny excitations lull me into a sort of torpor. I close my eyes over.

There is a yellow outline of a sea vessel riding across the waves of a broad bay that in parts is choppy and in parts is calm and in parts is heaving. There's nothing beyond the bay: no land, no markers of any kind. The tide of this sea is coming in, and the yellow outline of this large and seemingly unanchored vessel is being lifted onto wave after wave until it is gathered up and brought sliding and listing on the backs of some enormous waves into shore, where the vessel then tilts, reveals its outline-ness, crashes over and breaks apart into a multitude of yellow line elements. Then, from the centre of this breaking apart, out flood scores, then hundreds, then thousands more of these long yellow lines, line upon line, growing, surging, falling and dispersing onto the shore where they tumble and roll and flatten. More waves bend, crash and run up onto this dark shore where they push and pool around these spilt yellow lines, drawing them gradually back out into the white-edged surf until these lines then begin to fill out the bay, where they bob and bump soundlessly about, until, almost as quickly as they appeared, they submerge. I turn the volume down completely on both recordings as they enter into the second movement, played *andante*. I rise from my chair, leaving the two records spinning in quiet creaks on their turntables. Perhaps in a few hours' time or a few days' time I will make sense of what I have just listened to. Perhaps I will now listen to this piece of music only in this way, chasing its multitudes. Perhaps I have ruined this piece of music as a thing to be listened to separately. I walk down the corridor, past my bedroom on the left, the six succulent plants on my right and the door to my toilet on the left. Then I enter the kitchen and see out through the window the ivy rippling on the east-facing wall of our courtyard to a breeze passing down over itself in currents.

I STAND AT MY kitchen table and look out the window once more. I have taken my jacket from the back of the chair and I'm putting it on in preparation to leave the apartment for the day. It whisks as I move. It is a sky-blue wind-cheater, and I know by the time I get halfway to the museum I will be so warm that I will remove the jacket, ball it up and carry it in my hand until much later, when the breezes coming off the river begin to meet my back.

I look across the courtyard, and up to the top left-hand corner of the building opposite a flare of reflected white sunlight appears. The window must be streaky with residue of some kind, because it feels as though the light is fanning out towards me in rays. I wonder, at this time of morning, at this time of year, how the light can possibly be reflected in this direction. Then the window opens out fully and a young dark-haired woman appears. Her head is turned back into her kitchen as if she is talking to someone in the room. As she turns outwards, she produces a white tea towel and flicks it into air, shaking it out, as if she is releasing an unwanted insect or arachnid of some kind back into the outdoors. She flicks the white tea towel once more, then she seems to look directly down at me and the way she pauses while leaning out the window and flicking out the tea towel suggests to me that she is waving at me from the deck railing of a departing ocean liner, and for a moment I feel our two buildings slide a couple of inches apart. Then she flicks the towel out once more and continues to look, I feel, directly at me. I smile and from the darkness of my kitchen I wave back in a way that might be described as wan. She does not respond. I pull the zipper of my jacket halfway up and touch the left pocket to make sure that my keys are in there. I visualize the dark and patchily lit stairwell of my apartment block and the timber stairs curled around the rackety single-person lift that services the whole apartment building. I imagine the brightness and the fresh air when I step out onto Solokoexte. Then I look back out to this woman shaking out her tea towel, but she has just pulled her head and shoulders back into the darkness of her kitchen and she has taken in with her too the white tea towel she'd been waving at me not a few moments ago.

ACKNOWLEDGMENTS

Rice, Peter, *An Engineer Imagines* (Ellipsis London
Limited: London 1994)

Chomsky, Noam, *Cartesian Linguistics* (Cambridge
University Press: Cambridge 2009)

Leo, Maxim, *Red Love: The Story of an East German
Family* (Pushkin Press: London 2009)

Shiel, Michael, *The Quiet Revolution* (O'Brien Press:
Dublin 2003)

Builder Extraordinary: Ove Arup, dir. John Read, UK,
BBC TV 1966

Serra, Richard, *The Matter of Time* (Bilbao:
Guggenheim Museum 1997)

Allertz, Robert, *Im Visier die DDR. Eine Chronik*
(Edition Ost: Berlin 2002)

Foster, Hal, *The Art/Architecture Complex* (Verso:
New York 2011)

175

Thank you to Niamh Dunphy, Feargal Ward, Ruth Hallinan, Anna Benn, Kirstin Campbell, Saffron O'Sullivan, Gemma Kent and Amy O'Sullivan and thank you to my secondary-school teacher Pat Lynch – who first introduced me to world of descriptive and projective geometry.

My thanks also to the Arts Council of Ireland from whom I received a visual artist bursary, which helped greatly with the travel and research that became necessary as I wrote this novel.

Thank you to The Lilliput Press and especially to Antony Farrell whose encouragement gave me confidence. Finally, my thanks to Seán Farrell, who edited this book.